TRUSTING LOVE

A PARADOX LAKE SWEET ROMANCE

JEAN C. GORDON

UPSTATE NY ROMANCE

TRUSTING LOVE

*As always, much thanks to my critique group BFS (Chris, Colleen, and Thomasine)
and my editor Jena O'Connor.*

WELCOME TO PARADOX LAKE

*a*ny fan of sweet romance will love the stories of small-town love in the Paradox Lake Sweet Romance series. Grab your tea or coffee, settle into your favorite chair, and be swept away into the cozy Adirondack town where complex characters navigate challenging situations as they find their way to love. Whether it's love at first blush, old flames reuniting, or second chance romance, you'll find pure reading enjoyment and satisfy your craving for sweet, wholesome romance.

Part of an ongoing series full of familiar faces, each story will stand on its own. With novel and novella lengths available, there's something for everyone. Paradox Lake is written by *USA Today* Bestselling sweet romance author, Jean C. Gordon, who's penned stories for the No Brides Clubs Series, Indigo Bay Series, and Harlequin Love Inspired, as well as for multiple sweet romance collections.

CHAPTER 1

So that's what he's up to. Autumn Hazard skimmed through the article on her iPad. JMH Health Care had gobbled up another struggling nonprofit hospital in Upstate New York.

She ground her teeth. *If he thinks he's going to add the Ticonderoga Birthing Center to his family's collection, he had better think again.*

Autumn closed the article and went back to the list of not-yet-billed patients.

"Have you seen him?" Cindy, the birthing center's evening front desk manager, stood in the doorway to her office. "He's drop dead gorgeous."

Autumn rubbed her forehead. "Seen who?" As if she didn't know.

The middle-aged woman leaned against the door jamb as if in a swoon. "The new director."

Another woman fallen prey to his outward charms.

"Pretty is as pretty does," Autumn muttered. And nothing she'd seen Jonathan Mitchell Hanlon—nor his grandfather, the chairman of the board of directors of JMH—do was pretty.

"What?"

Autumn touched the screen to flip to the next page. "Something Great Grandma Hazard used to say."

"I've heard the saying. What I was questioning was your meaning. Wait, you know him."

"Yes, I worked with him briefly at Good Samaritan Hospital, when I was doing my midwife clinicals. He was an OB resident."

"Oh, then, you—" The sound of the door between the birthing suites and the lobby opening cut Cindy short. "I'd better get back out front."

"Good idea." Autumn picked up the printout of the directions for entering the insurance codes into the billing program. Their office assistant had gone and had her baby early, leaving Autumn and Kelly, the owner of the midwifery practice, without anyone lined up to fill in while she was on maternity leave.

Might as well get started. It wasn't as if she had any other Friday evening plans. Much as she loved living in her Adirondack Mountains hometown, Paradox Lake had a very limited supply of dateable men. A supply that had been made even smaller when Rod, the Navy recruiter she'd dated for several months, had been reassigned to a post in suburban Boston. She clicked the icon for the billing program. By entering the billing, she'd be making herself useful to the practice. A pang of regret jabbed her in the stomach. While Kelly had been understanding at first, what use was a midwife who couldn't bring herself to deliver babies?

Footsteps sounded in the hall.

"If your grandparents do come up to Lake George for a vacation, feel free to give them a tour of the center," the high-pitched voice of Liza Kirkpatrick, an administrator from the Adirondack Medical Center, carried clearly down the hall to Autumn's office.

Autumn tensed, listening for the response. All she heard was a deep rumble of indistinguishable words.

A minute later Liza was at the door to Autumn's office. "Autumn. Good, you're still here. I wanted to introduce our new director, Dr. Hanlon."

Liza and Jon stepped into her office. Cindy was right. Jon was gorgeous. If possible, even more so than when she'd last seen him. His dark hair was clipped a little shorter and neater than when he was a resident. His brilliant blue eyes still had that spark that hinted he knew something you didn't and invited you to try to find out what. And he'd obviously found time to get in his five-mile run every morning, or regular workouts at the gym. However, his classically symmetrical features had lost the harried look he'd always had back then. A look that had added to his appeal for many of the female staff members. They wanted to soothe his concerns away.

Autumn rose and stepped away from her desk. Jon gave her a charming smile that said he liked what he saw.

He doesn't remember me.

She certainly remembered *him*. She'd seen him use the same smile with every female he'd met at Samaritan Hospital.

The administrator introduced them. "Autumn Hazard, Dr. Jonathan Hanlon."

She took his extended hand, debating whether to let on that she knew him or let it drop. His grip was firm and businesslike.

"Good to see you. It's been a while." He released her hand. "Samaritan Hospital," he prompted as if she might have forgotten *him*.

"Yes, good to see you, too." Autumn shifted her weight

from one foot to the other as he studied her face. The seconds seemed to run into minutes.

He tilted his head. "I almost didn't recognize you. Your hair was different, shorter."

That was an understatement. When her long-time boyfriend had broken up with her on spring break, Autumn had had her waist-length hair cut in a short spikey style.

"Well," the administrator said. "It certainly is a small world. Autumn is one of two certified nurse midwives who deliver at the center and have an office here. We have one other midwife who has an office in Keene and splits her deliveries between the birthing center and the hospital in Saranac Lake."

"But," Autumn said, "I've taken a sabbatical from catching babies to develop the GYN side of the practice." At least that's what her official explanation was. Autumn didn't feel anyone at the birthing center, other than Kelly, needed to know that the complications at the last birth she'd attended had shaken her so much that Autumn wasn't sure when, if ever, she'd resume that part of the practice. It might have been less traumatic if the parents—Jack and Suzy Hill—weren't long-time friends.

Liza narrowed her eyes. Autumn knew the former birthing center director hadn't hesitated to make it clear to Liza and the rest of the hospital administrative staff that he wasn't pleased with Autumn's decision. It had potentially put him on call more often. Not that he'd actually been called more. There hadn't been more births than Kelly and the other midwife could handle.

"Is Kelly here?" Liza asked. She turned to Jon. "Kelly Philips is the other midwife Autumn works with."

"No," Autumn said. "One of our home-birth mothers went into labor a couple of hours ago. She and our delivery nurse Kari Evans are there."

Jon knit his brows. "The center condones home births?"

"We—"

Autumn interrupted Liza, bristling at the disdain in Jon's voice. "We're a private practice, so it's not up to the center to condone or not condone our mothers' birth arrangements."

"Autumn and Kelly and their two delivery nurses aren't employees of the birthing center," Liza explained in a placating voice. "The practice has privileges and leases space here."

Jon drew his lips into a hard line. "I assume the medical center's attorneys have vetted this arrangement for any liability that could come back on the center."

Autumn fisted her hands at her side. Jon's tone and words irritated her, even though she knew he was simply asking from a business standpoint. But it wasn't his concern how she and Kelly practiced. The practice's agreement was with the Adirondack Medical Center, not him.

"Certainly." Liza's terse reply was a sharp contrast to her earlier, almost fawning attitude.

Autumn flexed her fingers.

"And what's my responsibility if complications arise at one of these births and higher level medical intervention is needed?"

Shades of the former director? Was Jon concerned he'd have to do more than push paper? No. When she'd worked with him at Samaritan, he'd seemed to derive a lot of satisfaction out of delivering babies. But he'd had a technical approach to childbirth, almost like he was curing the mother of a deadly disease, rather than bringing a new life into the world. She bit her tongue to organize her thoughts, so she didn't blurt out the first response that had come to mind. It didn't work.

"With a normal birth, medical intervention isn't necessary."

Something flickered in his eyes that she would have normally read as pain. But that didn't make any sense.

"Even a seemingly normal birth can have complications."

Jon wasn't saying anything she didn't already know well. But most of their births didn't need the type of intervention he was talking about. "We continually screen our mothers and insist on a center delivery when we think one is needed or refer the mother to an obstetrician if we see anything abnormal that might require medical intervention or a hospital delivery."

"And when something goes wrong at home?" Jon asked.

"With our screening, that hasn't been a common experience." Her only life-threatening complication had occurred here at the center.

"You're saying that you've never had to rush a home-birth mother to the hospital?" he pressed.

Autumn silently counted to three. "We've had to transport a couple of laboring home-birth mothers to the birthing center."

He crossed his arms and nodded, as if her answer had proved some point.

Uneasiness washed over her. As director, Dr. Hanlon could initiate a review of her and Kelly's privileges here at the birthing center if he had a problem with their practice. The next closest medical facility, where they also had privileges, was an hour away at the Adirondack Medical Center in Saranac Lake. Autumn shook the feeling off. She was being paranoid. The center needed Kelly and her. The community needed them.

"We should get back to Saranac." Liza glanced from Jon to Autumn. "We have a dinner meeting with the board of directors of the hospital."

"Of course." Jon turned to Autumn. "I'll set up a staff

meeting for early next week and email you and your partner an invitation."

"The front office assistant has our patient schedule." No need to tell him she worked with Kelly under contract. He'd find out soon enough that she wasn't a partner.

"Good. I'll check with the office assistant." He took a step to follow Liza who was already at the doorway and stopped. His all-business expression softened. "You wouldn't by any chance be related to Neal Hazard at the campgrounds over on Paradox Lake?"

"Yes, he's my father. Why?" Autumn couldn't imagine any way Jon would know her father.

"I'm renting his duplex."

"The one on Hazard Cove Road?" He couldn't mean any other. It was the only duplex Dad owned. She'd assumed he was renting it to one of the usual families who took it for the summer.

"That's the one. I'll see you next week."

"Right."

Once he was out of sight, Autumn leaned against the edge of her desk. Dr. Hanlon was going to be her next-door neighbor. She could put her feelings about him and the thoughtless way he'd broken her Samaritan Hospital room-mate's heart behind her at work. She and Kelly practiced independently of the birthing center administration. And, since she'd taken leave from delivering babies, she was unlikely to have any need to consult with him as the practice's backup physician. If she made an effort, she could pretty much avoid him here.

But with him living right next door, avoiding him and keeping her dislike in check wouldn't be so easy. While she hadn't been bowled over by him like so many of the nurses, she'd liked Jon when she'd first met him and had half expected him to ask her out. But he'd asked out her roommate, Kate, instead. Then, after he'd broken up with Kate, he'd had the audacity to ask her out. And he'd seemed mystified when she'd turned him down. It hadn't taken him long to move on to another nurse friend, confirming the buzz around Samaritan that that he wasn't the settling down type. And, while it might seem old fashioned, she was.

Autumn pushed away from the desk, knocking a coffee mug of pens off the edge. Considering his reputation with women, he probably didn't remember any of it. But she did.

JON UNLOCKED the door and stepped into the front hall of the bed and breakfast in Crown Point where he was staying. He stretched the kinks out of his back as he climbed the stairs. What had been a pleasant hour drive from Ticonderoga to Saranac Lake in the bright summer evening hours had seemed interminable on the drive back in the dark. The distances people here in the Adirondacks had to travel for medical care were unbelievable compared to what he was used to downstate. And Liza had told him that Autumn and her partner's practice served a large part of the 60-mile distance between the birthing center and the hospital in Saranac, as well as some of the areas south of Ticonderoga.

He let himself into his room. Liza's comment had kept Autumn in his mind as he wound his way back to Crown Point. Thoughts of her traveling the steep narrow side roads he'd passed to deliver babies in homes set up on the mountainside alternated with visions of Autumn this afternoon, her delicate-featured face framed by wisps of flaxen hair escaping the silver clip that pinned the rest up.

As he slipped off his suit coat, he noticed the message light flashing on the phone. He was tempted to ignore it. Morning would be here all too soon, and he had to be up to meet the moving van at the duplex at eight. *That's it. It could be the movers.* He'd given the number here at the bed and breakfast as an alternate number where he could be reached.

Jon lifted the receiver and pressed the message button.

"Jay." His grandfather used the family nickname he'd dropped in middle school. "It's your grandfather. I'll be Upstate next week, and your grandmother insists on coming with me and having dinner with you. I've made reservations for Wednesday at six thirty at the Sagamore in Lake George."

The message clicked off with no goodbye. Typical of Grandfather. Bark an order and leave, fully expecting it to be obeyed without question. Jon dropped the receiver back in place. He should ignore it. Nothing he did pleased his family anyway. But he couldn't do that to Nana. Not after all she'd done for him. She'd provided the love his career- and stature-driven parents hadn't. She'd grieved and prayed with him when his favorite cousin and close friend Angela had died in childbirth in Haiti, where she and her fiancé had been serving with a nonprofit organization.

His parents' brief acknowledgement of his sorrow had been tinged with an undercurrent that it was punishment for Angie having conceived before she and her fiancé had married. Angie had gone through what his parents had viewed as a wild period at college. But by the time she and her fiancé had learned of the baby, those days were ancient history.

Jon's thoughts went to his cousin's husband, Brad, now raising their little boy alone. Jon jerked off his loosened tie. His anger at Angie's unnecessary death had grown into a need, a calling, to use his medical training and technology to do everything he could to protect other women and families from the same tragedy.

The directorship of the Ticonderoga Birthing Center was the perfect first step toward doing just that—maybe even more so now that he'd learned about some of the center's current practices. In his opinion, home births weren't something to be encouraged. Too many things could go wrong without emergency equipment on hand.

He tossed his tie on the dresser. Tightening up birthing center procedures shouldn't be too difficult. Part of the reason for the home births might be cost. Essex County had its share of lower income and uninsured people. That shouldn't mean mother and babies received less than optimal care. He'd check the center's financial records and work on Autumn and her partner, showing them his reasoning for technology-oriented care.

Back at Samaritan, he and Autumn had been friends of a sort, until Kate had alienated her and half the other staff by making her version of their breakup public—very public. Kate had known all along he wasn't serious about their relationship and, as far as he knew, she wasn't either. The disention she'd caused among the members of the medical team had been unacceptable.

He'd ignored the fracas as much as possible. And he'd done what he'd always done. Moved on. If he wanted conflict, he could visit his family.

CHAPTER 2

*a*utumn woke to the rumble of a truck engine, a truck much larger than her dad's or grandfather's pickup trucks. She checked her alarm clock—7:30—and dragged herself out of bed to the front window. A moving van sat running in the driveway. Jon was moving in today? She didn't even get a few days to acclimate to him at work before she had him here at home, too? She sighed. Jon was nowhere in sight. *Better go down and talk to the movers.*

As Autumn walked across her living room to the front door, she heard the crunch of another vehicle driving up the recently tarred and stoned road to the house. She waited at the door until she saw her stepmother Anne's SUV pull up in front.

"Autumn. We're here." Her three-year-old twin half brother and sister, Alex and Sophia, stated the obvious as they raced up the shared walkway, followed more sedately by their eight-year-old brother, Ian. The twins were still in their pajamas. Anne waved to her as she went to talk with the movers.

"Hi, guys." Autumn gathered the twins in her arms. "What's up?"

Sophia stood tall with an air of self-importance. "Daddy f'got to tell you. So Mommy and us had to come. Mommy is not happy."

Ian interpreted. "Saturday is Mom's day to sleep late 'cause she's teaching that morning class at the college during the week. It's my job to watch the twins and make sure they don't wake her up until 8:00." He pitched his voice to sound like watching his siblings was a big burden, but Ian's bright-eyed look gave away his pride that Anne trusted him with the responsibility. "Someone called, and the phone woke her up. She had to come to talk with the moving guys." He pointed at the van.

Autumn smiled over his head at her stepmother, who'd finished talking to the movers and was walking toward them.

"Hi," Anne said.

"Hi. I hear you're not happy."

Anne glanced at Sophia and laughed. "I'm never happy when I get woken up before I'm ready. I don't suppose your dad told you the new tenant was moving in today."

"No, Dad didn't even tell me he'd rented the place. I found that out at work yesterday."

"News does travel fast here."

"True, but I found out because the tenant is the new director of the center. Jon Hanlon. He told me."

"If it makes you feel any better, your dad didn't find out about the guy moving in until late last night. Since he's had so much out-of-town work this summer, he's left the rentals up to the realtor." Anne tilted her head. "I know he loves doing the solar electric installations, but his being out of town wreaks total havoc on my efforts to have a well-ordered life." She grinned. "Anyway, when the tenant couldn't get a hold of the realtor this morning, he called me and asked if I could let the movers know that he's on his way. He has to drive from Crown Point."

"You didn't have to come over. You could have called me."

"I know, but the house isn't your responsibility, and I didn't want to wake you up if you'd been out last night."

"I was. I had a hot date with a pile of billing invoices."

"Still haven't found a temporary office assistant?"

"No, but Kari texted me last night that she may have someone. Her cousin is looking for a summer job." Autumn motioned to the door. "So, do you have time to come in for a while? I'll put coffee on."

Anne looked longingly at the door. "No thanks. I told Drew I'd help with signing out this week's campers at Sunrise this morning. I need to get these guys home and dressed and down to the lake."

Autumn nodded. They all helped in the summer with the camp and conference center that her uncle Drew managed on her family's Paradox Lake property.

"But your aunt Jinx had better have some fresh coffee ready, or I'll leave this crew with her and be right back up the road to take you up on your offer."

"You're welcome anytime. I'm goofing off this morning. I'm on the crew to help with the cleanup and get-ready for the new campers coming tomorrow. So maybe I'll see you all later."

Autumn watched Anne fasten the kids in their car seats and drive away. She glanced at the moving van. The stony faced driver sat in the cab tapping the steering wheel with his finger while the other mover leaned against the side drinking a cup of coffee from the Paradox Lake General Store. She'd recognize the store's distinctive logo anywhere. It wasn't her problem that Jon was late. She went back inside and made some coffee for herself.

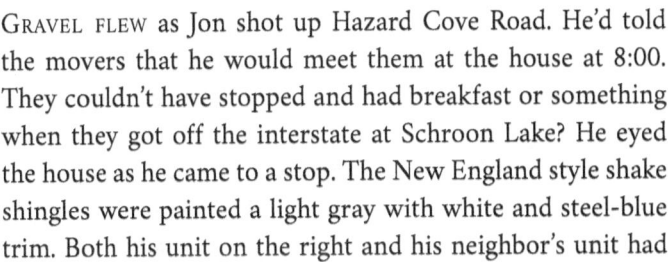

Gravel flew as Jon shot up Hazard Cove Road. He'd told the movers that he would meet them at the house at 8:00. They couldn't have stopped and had breakfast or something when they got off the interstate at Schroon Lake? He eyed the house as he came to a stop. The New England style shake shingles were painted a light gray with white and steel-blue trim. Both his unit on the right and his neighbor's unit had bright red front doors.

The realtor, who was the town historian, had talked his ear off about how the house dated back to the early 1800s and was built by one of the Hazards who'd settled the area for logging. He'd also regaled Jon with the details of how and when the current Hazard family members had built their homes on or just off Hazard Cove Road.

Jon got out of his car and strode across the yard to the moving van, wondering if those other family members included Autumn. Even though she was a few years younger than him, she might own a home.

The moving van driver and his helper got out and met him in front of the duplex.

"Dr. Hanlon?" the driver asked.

"Yes. Sorry for the delay. I wasn't expecting you until 8:00. I'll unlock the door."

The man nodded. "We'll start unloading."

Jon followed the shale walk up and to the left. He inserted the key the realtor had given him and swung the door in. A lemony scent mixed with the warm summer air. It and the gleaming wide planked pine floors attested to the realtor's word that he'd have the house cleaned and ready for him today.

"Hey, Doc." The helper wheeled Jon's Sportster down the

ramp and over beside the truck. "Sweet bike. Where do you want it?"

"In the back." The house didn't have a garage, but the realtor had assured Jon that there was plenty of room in the shake-sided out building behind the house. A former chicken coop, according to the realtor.

"Follow me." Jon led the mover to the shed and inserted the key the realtor had given him in the lock. It didn't work. He called the realtor and got his voicemail again, so he tried the Hazards' number. No answer there, either. A movement in the window of the other side of the duplex caught his eye.

"I'll go ask my new neighbor for a key." Jon crossed the yard to the back door and knocked. He tapped his foot as he waited for someone to answer.

"Hi."

"Autumn. You live here? I'm surprised the realtor didn't tell me. He told me the history and everything else there is to know about the house." Why was he stammering like the teenage nerd he once was facing the most popular girl at school? He looked into her light blue eyes. She probably had been one of the most popular girls at school—definitely one of the prettiest. "Why didn't you say something yesterday?"

"I thought I'd surprise you later once you were settled in."

The light in her eyes said she was teasing him, but years of sarcastic criticism from his family made him unsure whether he was reading her correctly. He cleared his throat. "Do you have a key to the shed? The one the realtor gave me isn't working."

"Yes, sorry about that. Some kids out partying tried to break into it a few weeks ago with a nail file that jammed in the lock. I don't know what they thought I had in there." She pushed an errant strand of hair behind her ear. "That's a problem here. There's not a lot to do, and some kids have too much time on their hands. I had to hacksaw the lock off and get a new one."

She spoke so matter of factly. "That didn't bother you, being out here alone?" He refrained from saying a woman here alone.

Autumn laughed. "Me, alone?"

Jon glanced around and saw nothing but pine forest. "Someone was living in the other unit?"

"No. But I'm surrounded by family. No one can get up the road without passing by Dad's and my grandparents' houses, and no one can come up from the lake without passing the lodge where my aunt and uncle live. I wasn't home, but Grandpa and Uncle Drew were both here in time to block the kids' car in. They ran off into the woods, but the sheriff's deputy caught up with them quick enough. They were summer folk. But you're not here for my life story. Come in and I'll get you the key."

Jon stepped in and waited in the kitchen for Autumn to return. He breathed in the aroma of the coffee brewing on the counter, and his stomach growled to remind him he hadn't had any coffee or breakfast.

"Here you go." Autumn walked back into the kitchen. She looked from him to the coffee maker he was eyeing and bit her lip. "Want a cup?" she asked after a moment.

"Yeah, but I shouldn't keep the movers waiting any longer than I have."

"I'll bring one out to you. Cream and sugar?"

"Black is good." He couldn't tell if she was being nice or wanted him to leave. "I really appreciate it."

"I could tell. You were looking at my coffee maker like a man who'd just crawled his way out of a waterless week in the desert."

"That bad?"

"That bad." She handed him the key on a key chain that

read, "I conquered the High Peaks."

Had she climbed all of the Adirondack High Peaks? he wondered. At Samaritan, she'd always been open to a challenge. His former roommate could attest to that. The roommate had run into Autumn and some of the other women shooting hoops at the Y one evening and, after some back and forth, had challenged them to a three-point competition. It had come down to his roommate and Autumn. She matched him shot for shot until the competition was called because the Y was closing.

So she certainly had the tenacity to conquer the peaks. Her crossed arms and wide-legged stance stopped him from asking, though. He should get back outside, but he couldn't seem to get his feet moving. They were going to be working together and living next door to each other. He'd like to get past the undercurrent of resentment she exuded.

"I'll bring the key right back."

"Keep it. I have another one, and you'll need a copy anyway."

He pushed open the screen door and reached behind him to close the main door.

"You can leave it open. It feels warm out already."

He looked up at the bright sun in the cloudless blue sky. "Yeah, it looks like a scorcher." As the aluminum door latched shut behind him, he wondered what had made him say that. *Scorcher.* It sounded like something they'd say on AccuWeather. And why was he so looking forward to Autumn bringing him coffee?

AUTUMN CARRIED two coffee mugs across the living room and opened the screen door with her elbow. Since the weather had warmed up, she often had her Saturday morning coffee outside on the patio Grandpa had added to her side of the house. She scanned the front yard. Neither Jon nor the movers were outside. She walked over to Jon's side and peered in the screen door. The living room was empty of people and furniture. The movers must have started with the upstairs furniture.

"Hello," she called, taking a sip of her coffee as she waited for a response.

Jon bounded down the empty stairway, opened the door and took the mug from her. He drank deeply. "Thanks. I really need this."

"You're welcome."

"I'd invite you to stay and drink your coffee with me, but I don't have a seat to offer you."

"That's okay. I was going to sit out on the patio. I don't want to keep you from your work."

"The movers can handle things. I'll join you if you don't mind."

She did mind. This morning was the only quiet time she expected to have all weekend. This afternoon, she was helping Drew at the camp. Gram and Grandpa had invited her for dinner tomorrow after church, and in the evening she was babysitting for her father and Anne so they could go out for their anniversary. She loved her family and everything that came with living close to them. But she'd hoped for a couple of hours to herself this morning.

Oh, well. It was her choice. She wouldn't trade living here at the lake for living anywhere else. At least not voluntarily. Autumn's throat constricted. Once her contract with Kelly was up in the fall, she might have to go somewhere else. She had her doubts that Kelly would offer her another contract if she still wasn't catching babies. And neither Adirondack Medical Center nor the Ticonderoga Birthing Center had staff midwives.

Jon smiled down at her with the smile that had made half the nursing staff at Samaritan go all weak and dreamy and the other half want to mother him like a favored son. Autumn had been an exception. Rather than wowing her like everyone else, Jon's masculine charms had irritated her. He'd been too smooth, too full of himself professionally and personally, although a few times when she'd seen him outside of work, she'd thought she'd glimpsed a different Jon underneath.

He motioned toward the walkway. "After you."

Autumn felt his eyes on her as she descended the porch steps. She wiped her palm on her denim shorts. She wasn't about to succumb to his charms now. Not unless he'd changed a lot in the past two years. And, from what she'd seen yesterday, he hadn't. She glanced toward the patio. They could finish their coffee and she'd still have some time before she had to be down at the lake to help Uncle Drew.

In two long strides, Jon was beside her on the walkway in front of her door.

"If you need a refill, I made plenty." *Not exactly the way to discourage him from hanging around.* She glanced at Jon out of the corner of her eye. But he was so right there. She'd needed to say something.

"That'd be great."

"Go ahead and I'll bring the pot out." What had gotten into her? Now she was offering to wait on him. Did her unsettled job situation have her so off kilter that she'd grasp at anything that made her feel useful?

Once Jon rounded the corner of the house to the patio, Autumn yanked her door open and stomped across her living room. She poured a couple of dollops of fat-free half and half in her cup, picked up the coffee pot and walked out to the patio as the calm, sane person she usually was.

Jon stood at the far edge of the patio looking up at the

roof. "I didn't notice the solar panels when the realtor showed me the place. Photovoltaic?"

"Yes. Dad put the system in last summer when he and Grandpa decided to divide the house into a two-family." Autumn placed the coffee pot and her mug on the round wooden table.

"By himself?" Jon's voice held a note of awe.

"More or less. It's what he does." Autumn sat on the circular bench and topped up her drink. While she knew her father's limitations, growing up as the only child of a teenage single father, she'd never completely outgrown her feeling that "Daddy could do anything" and was often surprised when people commented on his work.

Jon joined her and refilled his mug. "He owns a solar energy company or a construction company?"

For some reason, Jon's assumption that her father owned a company rankled. "Neither. He's a self-employed electrician, but he does hookups for several companies throughout the Northeast. It's Anne, my stepmother, who's the corporate tycoon of the family. She's the chairman of the board of directors of GreenSpaces and heads the environmental studies program at the college in Ticonderoga."

Autumn sipped her coffee while she waited for the name of Anne's international environmental engineering company to register with Jon and tried to figure out what she was doing. She didn't have to prove anything to Jon just because he came from a prominent old-money family.

He looked at her blankly over the edge of his coffee mug. "That's the community college I passed on State Route 74?"

Her coffee tasted bitter in her mouth. She should have brought the honey out. "Yes, North Country Community College. That's where I got my RN degree."

"You didn't go away to school? I couldn't wait to leave."

"I had an academic scholarship to Trinity College in

Chicago. My other grandfather was a professor there. But I just wasn't ready to leave home yet. I never knew my mother, and I'm not that close to him and my grandmother." She clamped her forefinger over her mouth. He didn't need —nor, probably, want—her family history, particularly since he wasn't sharing any of his.

Jon ran his gaze over the weathered shake siding of the house behind her, pausing at the drooping gutter knocked loose from the windstorm the week before last.

She glanced from the gutter to Jon and pressed her lips together. With his work getting the cabins ready for Camp Sunrise to open, Grandpa hadn't had a chance to repair the gutter. "A lot of the kids I went to high school with couldn't wait to leave, but I like it here at Paradox Lake. And it was a kick going to college with Dad. His electrician business had fallen off while he was serving in Afghanistan with the National Guard, so he took some environmental studies courses at NCCC while I was there. That's how he met Anne."

A warm gust of wind from the lake blew the gutter against the house with a thud, drawing Jon's gaze back to it.

Did he think it was going to fall on them? Or that Dad couldn't afford to hire someone to repair the gutter, hadn't had the money for her to go away to a big school? Autumn glanced from her empty mug to his newly refilled one to the drained coffee pot and wished she'd just given him his coffee and gone back inside to have hers.

No. She was being ridiculous, letting Jon push buttons she didn't even know she had. Maybe she hadn't had the privileged childhood that Jon must have, but she and Dad had done okay. She'd had as much as her friends.

He broke the silence. "It is beautiful up here. Relaxing. I can see why you came back after you finished your clinicals at Samaritan for your certification."

"That and family. We're close. And there's a need here for midwives, for almost any medical practitioner."

"True. The area is underserved."

"So that's what brought you up here?"

"Partly. But more the opportunity."

His reply jarred her. She'd thought she'd hit on something they had in common. A professional desire to serve where their skills were needed.

"There aren't a lot of places where someone my age can get the level of administrative experience that Adirondack Medical Center is offering me at the birthing center."

Maybe Jon had more in common with their last director than she'd thought yesterday. The center's former director had leveraged his experience at the birthing center into a cushy administrative position at a big medical center downstate.

Autumn shifted her weight on the bench. Jon could be grooming himself to take over his grandfather's health care corporation. The strains of a hit song by the local country band Forever Wild broke the growing silence.

"Excuse me." Jon pulled his cell phone from his pocket. His face lit when he saw the caller ID.

She pushed the bench back, ready to give him some privacy.

"Nana." Jon waved Autumn down as she started to rise. "Yes, we're on for dinner. I got the message." He frowned. "You don't have to apologize. See you then." He hunkered down over the phone. "Love you, too."

He shoved the phone back in his pocket. "My grandparents are going to be in Lake George Tuesday."

"Are they here on vacation?" Autumn remembered Liza, the medical center administrator, saying something yesterday about his grandparents vacationing in Lake George.

"No," he said brusquely. "Grandfather is coming up for a business meeting near Syracuse."

"Do you see them often?" After she'd babbled on about her family, it was only fair that he take his turn.

"No."

"Oh, I thought they might have lived near you. When you said coming up, I assumed you meant from the New York City, Westchester area."

He stared at her.

"That's where you're from, right, Westchester County?" From the gossip at Samaritan, she knew his father headed up the cardiology department at one of the medical centers there.

"Yes." He avoided eye contact. "I'd better get back to the movers." He stood and motioned toward the table. "Do you need any help carrying the stuff in?"

"No, thanks, I can handle it." So much for learning anything personal about Dr. Hanlon. Since as neighbors, they'd be seeing a lot of each other, she'd hoped he'd share something that might help her get past what he'd done to Kate and the cold way he'd treated his fellow hospital staff members afterwards. She picked up the mugs and coffee pot and walked with him to her door.

"I'll see you Monday."

She nodded and watched him cross the yard to the moving van before she went inside. Working with Jon and having him as her next-door neighbor was going to be interesting. The trouble was that, given their past history and the conversation they'd just had, Autumn had a sinking feeling it might not be a good kind of interesting.

CHAPTER 3

"*H*ello!" Her second-cousin Kari Evans's voice rang through the house to the kitchen.

Autumn put the clean coffee pot in the dish drainer and dried her hands with a dishtowel. "Hi, come in."

"I already am," Kari said from the doorway. "Who was that I passed on my way in? Tall, dark, and handsome. Talking with the moving guys." Autumn's friend and delivery nurse sighed.

"I thought you were more partial to the tall, fair-haired, and handsome type," Autumn teased.

"Don't tell the Colonel," Kari said of her husband, Eli.

"Your secret's safe with me. How'd you manage to slip out of the house alone?" Except for work, Autumn rarely saw Kari without Eli or one of the kids.

"Myles is at the camp."

"That's right. He's a counselor this summer."

"Rose slept over at a friend's, and Eli took Opal with him to the hardware store in Ticonderoga to buy new tile for the kitchen floor. But you're evading my question."

"The mystery man you saw on your way in is my new neighbor and boss, Dr. Jonathan Hanlon."

Kari tilted her head. "Boss?"

"The new director at the birthing center. Technically, not our boss, but something tells me he's going to be a lot more hands on with the actual care than Dr. Ostertag was. I worked with Jon at Samaritan when I was doing my master's degree."

"I see." Kari's eyes twinkled.

"You see nothing. Just because I know him doesn't mean I like him."

"So you don't like him?"

Autumn threw up her hands and laughed. "I didn't say that, exactly. I don't know him that well." Nor did it look like he'd be an easy person to get to know.

"It's been a couple of months since Rod was reassigned."

Autumn shook her head. "I know you'd like everyone to be as happy and in love as you and Eli are, but my time hasn't come yet. Now, you must have had a reason for stopping by, other than trying to fix me up with Jon—especially since you didn't even know about him until you got here."

"You're not going to go for it, then?"

"I'm not going to go for it."

Kari released an exaggerated sigh. "I know you're helping out at the camp today, too. So I stopped in to see if you want to walk to the lake with me." She patted her slightly rounded belly. "My midwife says that I need to get some more exercise. Apparently, chasing the other three kids around isn't enough."

"Using my words against me?" Even though Autumn wasn't taking on any obstetric patients, when Kari had found out she was pregnant, she'd insisted on seeing Autumn for her prenatal care. Their friendship went back a long time to when Autumn was a high school student and used to babysit Kari's older kids.

"Come on, you weren't planning on driving down. You walk everywhere."

"You're right. I was going to walk." But she'd planned on having the morning to herself. Autumn kicked off her sandals and picked up her sneakers from the rug by the door. "Let me change my shoes and we can go."

"Sure, and while I'm thinking of it, my cousin who I texted you about would be happy to fill in at the office for the summer. She's still working on getting a teaching position for the fall and has to be out of her apartment in Syracuse by the end of the week. She really doesn't want to go back to her father's in Buffalo."

Autumn looked up from tying her shoes.

"They get along great. But Uncle Steve recently remarried, and Lexi, short for Alexandra, thinks her father and stepmother have enough with her new teenage stepbrothers there."

"I can relate to that." Autumn stood.

"I thought you could." Kari grinned.

"Do you think Lexi would be interested in the trivia group? Our ranks have thinned lately."

"Maybe. I'll ask her. Is that a prerequisite for the job?"

"Of course not. I was just thinking we need to get the group pumped up. You could tell her it's the closes thing Paradox Lake has to a singles group, although about half our members are married,"

Kari cocked her head to the side. "Back on topic. So, does Lexi have the job?"

Autumn thought about the hours she'd spent yesterday evening entering all of the billing into the computer. "I'll have to talk with Kelly, but I think she'll trust your recommendation."

"She'd better be able to. Seriously, I think you'll like Lexi a lot. And, back to the trivia group. What about your new neighbor?"

"What about him?" Autumn asked, even though she knew exactly what Kari was asking.

"Would he be interested in joining your group? You're down one on the male members since Rod left."

Autumn shrugged. "As I said, I don't know him that well." Besides, when had it become *her* group? And, even if the trivia group did need members, particularly male members, she had enough qualms about her and Jon getting along working together and as neighbors without adding him to the only regular social life she had.

Jon shook his head and put his helmet back on. No one had been home at either of the Hazard family houses. He'd even swallowed his pride and tried Autumn's. How could he have locked his house key in the duplex? He didn't do things like that. But the movers had been trying right from the start, getting there early. And his grandmother's call and Autumn's questions about his family had unsettled him. He understood that she was only making conversation. But he didn't talk about his family. Didn't think about them if he could avoid it, except for Nana.

He settled himself on his Sportster and revved it up to drive down to the lake. Hopefully, he could search out Autumn's grandfather or stepmother for a key and not have to share his stupidity with her. Although why should it matter? It wasn't like he was out to impress her or anything. Jon gunned the engine and gravel flew out from the rear tire, causing the bike to fishtail. He slowed down and reached the camp at a more sedate pace.

As he drove under the sign welcoming him to Camp Sunrise, a group of high-school and college-age kids crossing the parking lot with mops, buckets and other cleaning items stopped and stared. He rolled to a stop and kicked down the stand. By the time he'd pulled off his helmet, a couple of the boys were beside him.

"Nice ride," the dark-haired one said.

"Yeah," his companion echoed.

"I'm Myles Hazard, one of the camp counselors. You need directions or something?"

Ah, another Hazard family member. "I'm looking for Anne Hazard or her father-in-law."

"Mr. Hazard just left for the store. He probably passed you on the road."

Jon nodded. A pickup had gone by him.

"I'm not sure where Anne is, but I'll get Autumn, her stepdaughter. She can probably help you."

"That's okay." He lifted his helmet to put it back on. He didn't have Mr. Hazard's phone number, but he could leave Anne a message at the number he'd called this morning. Then he could kill some time at his office in the birthing center preparing for the staff meeting next week. "I'll catch up with Mr. or Mrs. Hazard later."

"It's no problem. Autumn's right over there on the lodge porch."

He followed Myles's outstretched arm to the large log building next to the parking lot where Autumn was walking down the stairs. Jon weighed which was more asinine, his insisting on not talking to Autumn or his reluctance to tell her he'd locked himself out.

Myles relieved him of the decision. "Hey, Autumn, this guy needs to talk to you."

Autumn turned quickly, causing her almost waist-length

ponytail to swing over her shoulder. She waved an acknowl-edgement.

A feeling of protectiveness waved over him as she approached. He turned to the boys. "I know you're trying to help, but you don't know who I am."

They looked at him blankly. "Should we?" Myles's friend asked.

Was he that clueless when he was a teen? Probably. "I could be anyone. You don't know that Autumn knows me."

"Hi, Jon."

The teen looked from him to Autumn. "But she does."

"Never mind, and thanks for the help."

"What was that about?" Autumn asked.

"I was looking for your grandfather or stepmother, and the dark-haired one, Myles, immediately volunteered to get you, without asking who I was or what I wanted."

"They're 15. They were probably too interested in your bike to remember their elementary school stranger-danger training."

Jon didn't know why her blithely dismissing his concern irritated him. What did it matter?

"You were looking for Grandpa or Anne. Is there a problem at the house?"

"Kind of." He dropped his gaze and tapped his helmet against his thigh. "I seem to have locked myself out."

Autumn made a soft choking sound and he looked up to see her lips twitch as she tried to contain her smile.

"I don't suppose you have a key to my side of the house."

Her smile broke through. "No, I don't. Anne probably does at the house. Come on, I'll take you to her. You can leave your helmet. It'll be fine. I'll tell Myles to keep an eye on it and your bike. They're done cleaning the campers' cabins."

He surveyed the forest surrounding the parking lot and the kids milling around the camp and held on to the helmet.

A tow-headed boy of about three charged at them when they entered the lodge. "Aunt Autumn. You came back."

She scooped him up before he collided with Jon. "Silly Sam." She rubbed noses with the toddler. "Of course I came back. I said I would."

"Your nephew?" He didn't know Autumn had any brothers or sisters. Then, why should he?

"No, Sam is my cousin. He belongs to my aunt Jinx and uncle Drew. Drew is the camp director. But Sam decided that if Anne is Aunt Anne, I should be Aunt Autumn."

The little boy nodded and pointed to a group of women talking on the other side of the room. "Aunt Anne."

One of them looked like a slightly older, taller version of Autumn, right down to the long blond ponytail, or in her case, braid. Another was an attractive woman with light brown hair who looked about his age, thirtyish. The third woman was older, probably, Anne, Autumn's stepmother. Numerous children, all too young to be campers, surrounded the women.

"Who are you?" Sam asked.

Jon shoved his free hand in the front pocket of his jeans. Aside from the babies he delivered, children were alien creatures to him. "I'm Doc...Jon."

"Uncle DocJon?" Sam faced Autumn waiting for her answer.

A blush spread across her face and Jon noticed a light spattering of freckles on her patrician nose that he hadn't noticed before.

"No," she said. "Just Jon or Doctor Jon." She looked at him for confirmation.

He nodded. He'd been taught to address adults by Mr. or Mrs. or Doctor So and So, in the case of his parents' associates. But it wasn't like he was going to be seeing the kid on a regular basis.

"Sam has also decided that adults should come in pairs—mommies and daddies and grandmas and grandpas and aunts and uncles."

"Oh." That sounded brilliant, but he didn't know what else to say. He looked pointedly at the group of women across the room, who were now moving toward them with a stream of kids behind. He should have just gone to his office at the birthing center.

Autumn waved them on. "Everyone, this is Doctor Jonathan Hanlon, the new director at the birthing center." She went around the circle introducing the women as her aunt, grandmother, and Anne—not stepmother—and identifying the various children ending with, "These are my brothers, Ian and Alex, and my sister, Sophia."

"Call me Jon, please." He felt a tug on his pant leg.

The little girl Autumn had introduced as her sister stood beside him, hands on hips. "Are you Autumn's new boyfriend?"

"Sophia," Anne cautioned.

Autumn seemed to be studying the laces of her sneakers.

"What? I was just asking." Sophia raised her big blue eyes to him. "Autumn's old boyfriend had to move somewhere else, and she was sad. She needs a new boyfriend."

Jon coughed. He didn't think that was a position he was going to step into. When he'd asked Autumn out at Samaritan, she'd shot him down with a terse, "No, thank you."

"No, Sophia, he's not my new boyfriend. He works at the birthing center with me. I told you that when I have a new boyfriend, you'll be the first to know."

"'Cause we're sisters."

"Yep, because we're sisters."

"Sorry about that," Anne said.

Obviously, the Hazard family didn't subscribe to the "children should be seen and not heard"—or better yet not seen and not heard—tenet he'd been raised with.

"Did you get all moved in?" Close up Anne looked a little older than he had originally thought, but not old enough to be Autumn's mother.

Like many of his father's colleagues, Autumn's father apparently had gone with a younger wife the second time around and a second family. He attributed his parents' adherence to their marriage vows to the fact that they rarely saw each other. That and their passion to out-accomplish each other. His father couldn't be happy sharing his mother's research breakthroughs. He had to offset them with a new surgical procedure—and vice versa. To avoid anything resembling his parents' relationship, Jon had made a pact with himself never to date other doctors.

He shook off the memories and answered Anne's question. "Yes. Thanks for alerting the movers that I was on my way."

"But he has another problem," Autumn said. "He's locked himself out. Dad must have another key at the house."

He glared at Autumn. She couldn't have pulled Anne aside and asked?

"We did," Anne said. "But Alex flushed it down the toilet."

"Sophie dared me do it," Alex said as if that explained the matter.

"You tried the realty office?" Anne asked.

"Yes, I left a message there and on the realtor's cell phone. I'm surprised I haven't heard back."

"He's probably out showing a property. If you haven't noticed yet, cell phone coverage can be very spotty here. My father-in-law should have a key. Mary?" She turned to her mother-in-law.

"He does," Autumn's grandmother said. "It's on his key

chain. He'll be back any time. He went to the hardware store and is going to stop and pick up pizza for everyone. You're more than welcome to stay and have some with us."

After spending the day helping the movers, he'd thought he'd take a bike ride, which he had, get some takeout and relax in front of the TV. He glanced around the noisy room. Relax alone.

Autumn locked his gaze with hers. "We may be a little much for Jon." She motioned around the room. "The kids and all."

He tensed. She didn't think he could handle them. Jon imagined eating with the kids. Tomato sauce, spilled drinks, grubby fingers. He pasted a smile on his face. "Sounds good, thanks. While I wait, I think I'll go check out the lake." He wasn't going to let a few kids intimidate him. If his father had taught him anything, it was that a Hanlon never showed weakness.

AUTUMN WATCHED Jon stride across the room and out the door. The speed at which he left confirmed her feeling that he'd been uncomfortable with her large, noisy family. She'd been certain he'd go off to a corner to wait for Grandpa, get his key and go back to the duplex. She had no idea why he'd agreed to stay.

A minute later, the screen door to the lodge pushed back open. "Was that who I think it was heading down to the beach?" Kari's voice carried across the room. "You had a change of heart?"

Autumn felt her family members' eyes on her.

"Go ahead down to the lake if you want, honey," Grandma said. "We really are done."

Just what she didn't need. The other women in her family

joining in with Sophie and Kari to try and fix her up with Jon.

"Eli," Autumn said to the tall man who'd followed Kari in with her daughters beside him, "can't you do something with her?"

"No, not a thing. Why, what's she up to?"

"Matchmaking."

Kari shook her head. "I'm encouraging her to get to know the new director of the birthing center better. We passed him on our way in."

Autumn's aunt Jinx caught her attention and rolled her eyes. At least someone was on her side. Maybe she should head home and catch the alone time she'd planned on this morning.

"Pizza delivery," Grandpa's voice boomed from the lodge porch, taking care of that decision.

"I'll open the door," Ian said, racing across the room.

She smiled. Anne was strict about what she let the kids eat, so pizza was a real treat for Ian. That had to have been a change for Dad, who'd pretty much figured in pizza as one of the three major food groups when Autumn was growing up.

"Go let your friend know food is here," Gram said.

Her friend. Like she was Ian's age. No, she was being too sensitive. As she passed by Grandpa, the spicy smells of the pizzas made her stomach growl, reminding her that all she'd had to eat today was the coffee with Jon and a granola bar she'd grabbed from the camp kitchen mid-afternoon. That would explain a lot of her crankiness.

"I'll be right back," she called over her shoulder as the door swung closed behind her. "Save some of the veggie pizza for me."

"You can have it all," Ian said, and everyone laughed.

Autumn paused on the porch. Jon could be anywhere along

the lakeshore, so she headed to the most obvious spot—the camp swimming dock. The evening sun filtering through the trees made an interesting shadow pattern on the wide gravel path to the lake. When the dock came into view, she raised her hand over her eyes to block the sun and scanned its length for Jon. He wasn't there. *Fabulous*. Her stomach growled again.

"Jon, pizza's here." Her voice echoed over the still water. She looked up and down the length of the camp's waterfront as she listened for a response. She didn't see or hear anything. Maybe he'd gotten tired of waiting and left. Except his bike helmet was up at the lodge, and she didn't think he'd be that rude. More likely, he'd decided to take a run along the beach. He could be halfway around the lake. And she wasn't about to hike the circumference looking for him.

Walking toward the dock, she spotted one of the megaphones the camp lifeguards used. She flicked the battery switch. "Jon, pizza." This time her voice boomed over the lake, and she caught a motion to her right.

Jon jogged over to her. "That's some voice you've got."

She lifted the megaphone. "Me and Amplivox. You didn't hear me the first time?"

He shook his head and gazed out at the water. "It's so quiet here. I'm surprised I didn't. But I was a ways up the beach."

"Quiet for now. Wait until tomorrow when the new campers arrive. That will make the family crew up at the lodge look like nothing."

He frowned.

"So you admit it. You found the family a little intimidating."

"I admit to nothing." A smile tugged at the corners of his mouth. "You didn't happen to bring the pizza with you, did you?"

"No, I did not. But my brother Ian is saving some of the veggie one."

"I'm more of a meat lover's fan myself."

Of course he was.

"Autumn, Autumn." Ian raced up to them. "You have a phone call."

"Do you know who it is sweetie?"

"Your friend Kelly. She talked to Opal's mother, but she wants to talk to you."

Autumn turned to Jon. "It might be one of our mothers, although we don't have anyone due for a couple of weeks." She hurried ahead to the lodge.

Kari handed her the lodge phone. "Kelley said to call her back on her cell phone."

Autumn dialed the number and listened while Kelly explained the situation. "Okay, I'll need to stop by my house. See you in a bit. Bye."

She placed the phone on the table. "Sorry, Gram, Aunt Jinx. I have to go. Oh, Jon, did you get your key?"

"Yes. Is there a problem with one of your mothers?"

"No, come outside."

They stepped out onto the porch. "Kelly got a call from one of her friends. The woman's daughter is in labor and she's afraid something isn't right. The couple is free birth. They were determined to have their baby with no interference from anyone. But the woman has talked them into letting Kelly come."

"Free birthers. The mother-to-be hasn't had any prenatal care?"

"Not that I know of."

"I'll go ahead to the birthing center and make sure one of the rooms is ready."

"Jon, we're not sure the couple will even let us help with

the birth. I doubt we can talk them into coming to the center."

"Insist. You said the mother thought something was wrong." Jon crossed his arms.

Autumn mirrored his stance. "We can't make them go to the center." She dropped her arms. There was no need to turn this into a standoff. Besides, this wasn't her birth. It was Kelly's. Kelly was in charge. Autumn swallowed the guilt that waved over her and didn't try to distinguish whether it came from her not holding up her end of the practice work or the relief she'd felt because Kelly was in charge. How long would Kelly agree to go on managing all of the deliveries?

He placed his hand on her forearm. "You have to try to get them to the center."

Kelly's van rolled into the camp parking lot. Autumn gently pulled away. "No, I have to go help catch a baby."

"I'll expect a report on Monday."

Autumn strode to the van and climbed in.

"Who is that?" Kelly asked.

"That's right. You haven't met him. He's Jon Hanlon, the new director of the birthing center."

"Oh. What does he want you to report?"

"Our business."

Kelly creased her forehead in question.

"I don't know why, either. But whatever his reason, I don't think I'm going to like it."

Like she didn't like the way he'd said they had to get the mother to the birthing center, didn't like him expecting her to report in to him on Monday and didn't like the way he seemed to think all he had to do was smile and he'd get his way.

CHAPTER 4

*J*on tested the doorknob to the midwifery practice. It had been locked when he'd tried it on his way to his office earlier. This time the knob turned. He hesitated. He'd exercised great restraint yesterday morning by not going over to Autumn's place to ask about her unexpected delivery on Saturday. Her car hadn't been in the driveway when he'd gotten up but had been an hour later. After giving her a few hours to catch up on her sleep, he'd glanced out and she'd been gone again.

Today, he had the good excuse of wanting to introduce himself to Kelly, along with finding out how the delivery had gone. He pushed the door open and looked around the empty waiting area. Two warm brown leather couches in the corner framed an oval coffee table, forming an inviting sitting area. Matching leather chairs were positioned a couple of feet away along the wall, one on each side of a combination table magazine rack. A desk sat on the opposite side of the room, and paintings of a mountain scene and the monthly stages of pregnancy hung on the wall in between.

He walked over and checked them out. They were both done by the same artist, probably a local.

"Can I help you?"

Jon turned.

"Dr. Hanlon?"

He nodded.

"It's good to finally meet you," the attractive middle-aged woman with auburn hair said. "I saw you briefly at the lake on Saturday."

He glanced behind her down the short hall. "You must be Kelly."

"Yes." She extended her hand. "Kelly Philips. Good to meet you. I would have introduced myself when I picked up Autumn, but I was kind of in a hurry."

"Understandable." He shook her hand. "And call me Jon."

The office door opened, and Autumn's voice rang out. "I've got coffee."

Jon tightened his grip on Kelly's hand, prompting a raised eyebrow from her. He quickly released it.

Autumn backed into the room. "I have your latte, a large regular for Kari and my mocha. She turned around, and the cardboard tray dipped dangerously to one side. "Jon."

"Good morning."

"Hi." She righted the tray and handed Kelly her coffee.

"I stopped in to introduce myself to Kelly and see how your delivery went on Saturday."

"It was really Kelly's delivery." Autumn looked to the other midwife. "Is Kari getting the exam room ready? I'll take her coffee to her."

"I'll take it, although I don't know if either of us will be able to enjoy the coffee. Our 9:30 appointment called and asked if she could come at 9:00." Kelly checked her watch. "I heard the door open and close and came out to see if she was here and found Jon."

Autumn lifted her mocha and handed the tray with Kari's coffee to Kelly.

"Why don't you take Jon to your office and fill him in on the birth while I get ready for my appointment?" Kelly said.

Autumn pressed her lips into a pink-tinged slash.

Jon set his jaw. Evidently, talking with him was that distasteful.

"Maybe he'd like to go with you on your home visit with the new mother this morning," Kelly said.

"Was there a problem?" he asked. Autumn had said Saturday that she didn't know whether the mother had had any prenatal care.

"No." Autumn drew out the O. "Why?"

"The home visit. Or do you do that with all of your home births?"

The office door opened, and a visibly pregnant young woman in a calf-length navy blue skirt and three-quarter-length-sleeved white cotton maternity t-shirt walked in, followed by two little girls. Jon guessed they were about two and three. The little girls were dressed in matching sun dresses with white t-shirts underneath.

"Hi," the woman said. "Am I seeing you, Kelly or Autumn today?" She dropped her gaze as soon as she noticed him.

He'd have to ask Autumn if this was a family from the traditional religious sect his delivery nurse had told him about. Apparently, Dr. Ostertag had experienced problems with a couple of the families because they insisted on using only midwives or a female doctor. He'd had concerns about an emergency arising when he was the only doctor available. Fortunately for Dr. Ostertag, none had.

"You'll be seeing me," Kelly said. "Let's make sure your information is up to date." She and the mother-to-be stepped over to the desk.

"My office is this way." Autumn turned heel, leading Jon

down the short hall. "Getting back to your question, we make a home visit after all of our births, even the ones here at the center." She halted at the last door on the right.

He didn't know what he'd said to prompt the irritation in her voice. He was interested in the extra degree of care. "That must involve a lot of time. Have you found it cost-effective in the long run?"

She pushed the door open and motioned him to a couch that matched the ones in the waiting room. A coffee table was positioned in front of it. He sat at the far side. She placed her mocha on the table, opened the messenger bag slung over her shoulder to remove her iPad and sat at the opposite end.

"I haven't done a cost analysis. Kelly may have. It's her practice.

Autumn worked for Kelly? That surprised him. He'd assumed she was a partner since Autumn had always said she wanted to practice near her hometown.

I'm sure she'd be happy to share it with you if she has." Autumn touched the iPad screen to open her notes.

Jon pulled a paper pad and pen from his pocket. He knew digital medical records and notes were the way, but he still preferred pen and paper for his personal notes.

She rattled off the details of the birth while he scribbled on the paper.

He looked up. "The Apgar scores assessing the baby's physical condition?"

"Seven at birth, eight at five minutes, and nine at ten minutes." Autumn read the results of test.

As HE RECORDED the Apgar scores, Autumn couldn't help feeling he was scoring her, too. On what, she wasn't sure.

She tried to read the rest of his notes, but the combination of reading upside down and his handwriting made them indecipherable.

"I like that you did the third test. Seven isn't a bad score, but you can't be too careful with a new life."

Or a mother's life, Autumn thought, a flashback to her friend Suzy's delivery filling her mind.

"You don't agree?" he asked.

"No." She cleared her throat. "I mean yes, I agree." For the first time since he'd arrived in Ticonderoga.

"You frowned." He shook his head. "Never mind."

Autumn closed her notes. "That's it." She waited for him to stand and leave.

"About that home visit Kelly mentioned—"

"I understand if you have other things to do."

"Nothing I can't do later. What time are you leaving?"

She checked her watch. "In about 20 minutes. They live a half hour away, and the visit will take a couple of hours."

"That long?"

Autumn's mood lightened. The visit would take up the whole morning. This was his first official day on the job. Surely, he couldn't give up that much time. "More or less."

Jon pressed his lips together as if trying to come up with a response.

She suppressed a smile waiting to hear how he'd work his way out of going on the home visit with her.

"You'll have to drive," he said. "I rode my bike."

Her thoughts jumped to her clutter-strewn car. As if it mattered. She didn't need to impress him. But he would need to sit somewhere. "I know. I heard you take off."

His eyes sparked and the corner of his mouth tugged up.

A tingle started in her stomach and bubbled through her giving Autumn an inkling of why all of the female staff at Samaritan Hospital had fawned over him. *No!* She mentally doused the feeling. She was not about to become the newest member of the Jonathan Hanlon fan club.

"I was up getting ready for work. I couldn't help but hear." It wasn't as if she was keeping track of his comings and goings if that's what he thought.

Jon stood. "I'll see you in twenty minutes."

"Meet me in the parking lot." That would give her a chance to move the towels and swim gear she'd stashed in the front seat to the trunk and toss out the remnants of her fast-food breakfast and miscellaneous trash. She had the twins' car seats in the back since she was picking them up at daycare today for Anne on her way back from the home visit and taking them to the lake. "The blue Kona."

"I know."

She warmed before it struck her. Of course he knew. Her car had been parked in front of the duplex for most of the weekend. "Right."

He let himself out of the office and Autumn went in search of a plastic trash bag—ditching the brief thought she'd had of ducking into the ladies room to touch up her makeup and check her hair.

JON PUSHED the back door to the birthing center open to see Autumn standing by her car stuffing things into a canvas bag with a mountain logo on it. The morning sun brought out silvery highlights in her pale blond hair. She set the bag on the pavement next to a white plastic bag and leaned into the open door. When she stood, she had two swim noodles in one arm and an inner tube in the other. She tossed the noodles over the seat into the back of the car and pressed her key tag to open the trunk.

"Need a hand?"

Autumn dropped the tube and it rolled toward Jon. He caught it and walked it back to her.

"You want it in the trunk?"

"Yeah, but I'll have to rearrange a few things first." She brushed by him and lifted the back hatch door, standing to one side as if she wanted to block his view of the storage area.

His curiosity got the best of him, and he stepped behind her and peered over her shoulder. "Interesting collection of equipment," he said taking in the jumble of toys, a beach bag, her oxygen tank, an orange EMT bag with a stethoscope looped over the top of one pocket and an inflatable birthing pool mostly folded into its "Birth-in-a-Bag" canvas container.

Pink tinged her cheeks as she made room for the inner tube, reminding him of the wholesome touch of innocence that had first attracted him to her when they'd met at Samaritan Hospital. It was that quality that had prompted him to ask her roommate, Kate, out, rather than Autumn. Kate was more of a party girl. He knew she wouldn't expect anything long term and that observation proved true. Contrary to the scuttlebutt that had spread through the Labor and Delivery wing, his breakup with Kate bruised her ego far more than her heart.

Autumn had struck him as a long-time kind of woman, and he'd known they both were at Samaritan temporarily. That thought had made it easier on him when she'd turned him down when he'd asked her out. He'd known that his timing wasn't right, but there was something about Autumn that had compelled him to ask anyway.

"There." She stepped back, causing him to jump out of the way.

He hadn't realized how close together they were standing.

She waved over the cleared-out spot next to the beach bag. "I have to pick the twins up from daycare on my way home and take them to their swim lesson at the lake. Anne has a web conference after her class this morning."

Jon bit back a smile, getting a bittersweet kick out of the easy way Autumn went on about her family without knowing she was doing it. He lifted the tube into the car, and she closed the hatch.

Autumn got in and started the vehicle. "The visit is up in Schroon Falls. If you've driven Route 9 from the medical center in Saranac Lake, you've gone through it."

"No, I've always taken the interstate."

"The Northway is a lot faster."

His mind went back to Friday when the drive to Crowne Point had seemed interminable on the interstate Autumn called the Northway. "I take it your visit this morning isn't off the interstate."

"Right, but unless time is a real factor, I tend to avoid the Northway. I get that from my dad. He never takes a highway if he can take a byway. It drives Anne crazy sometimes."

He could see that. In the case of these home visits, unnecessary time on the road would mean less time with that patient or another patient or in the office. "But you take the interstate when you're called for a delivery." He figured that was a given.

She shrugged. "It depends. We usually have time."

Jon shifted in his seat. She seemed so nonchalant about it. As he was all too aware, a birth could be a life and death situation. Of course, rural Upstate New York wasn't rural Haiti. He looked out the window at the mountain rising to his right. But it wouldn't be unusual for a home-delivery patient's house to be an hour from lifesaving equipment at the birthing center or the medical center in Saranac Lake.

The natural break in their conversation drew out into a

lull that made the drive time drag. *Might as well check in with the office.* He pulled out his smartphone and touched the mail app, tapping the side of the phone while he waited for it to open. It took a moment for him to notice the no-signal icon in the right-hand corner.

"Do you often have trouble getting reception around here?"

"All the time," Autumn said. "It doesn't matter which service you use."

"That could be a problem."

"If you need to make a call, I'm sure Megan would let you use her house phone. We'll be there in five minutes."

"It's not important. I was trying to check my office e-mail. What I meant was for being on call."

"It can be challenging. No one around here depends solely on a cell phone. Kelly and I give our expectant parents our home landline numbers and our cell numbers, in addition to the office number. If I'm at Dad's or Aunt Jinx's or a friend's, I'll often set my cell phone to forward my calls there to make sure I get them. Of course, the birthing center's off-hours answering service has all of our numbers."

Jon couldn't imagine giving his former practice's service a friend's phone number or any of his family members' numbers, even if he were close to them. It seemed unprofessional. "I guess that's the best you can do. A pager service wouldn't work any better."

Autumn's expression hardened. "It isn't that big of a deal. People get a hold of us. Neither Kelly nor I have missed a birth yet."

He couldn't shake the thought that they could, or he could, and of the possible consequences. His cousin had died because she didn't have a doctor at her birth to manage the complications. "I'd better call the phone company and have the landline connected.".

"Good idea. The house we're going to is right up here." Autumn turned left on Peaks Hill Road and followed it to the end, stopping in front of a small boxy house.

He looked at the solar collectors on the roof. "Your dad's work?"

She wrinkled her forehead in puzzlement. "Oh, the collectors. No. Dave, the new father, said he'd bought the system online and installed it himself. He's interested in talking with Dad."

Jon's gaze went from the gleaming collectors to the blistered peeling paint on the cottage and the dip in the wooden step to the front door.

"Ready?" she asked, swinging her door open.

He followed suit and stepped out of the car, walking around to meet her at the trunk.

She clicked the hatch open and grabbed her stethoscope from the EMT bag and a black and white pull-behind suitcase with pink hearts and a cartoon cat on it.

He tried to keep a straight face.

"Hello Kitty." Autumn nodded at the bag. "My sister, Sophie, picked it for my last birthday. She thought my brown one was too dull."

"That one isn't dull." He let the smile spread across his face and received a matching one from Autumn. His heartbeat ticked up a notch. He pulled his gaze from her and perused the trunk. "Need anything else?"

"Yes, can you grab the scale? It's there under the inner tube."

He reached under the tube for the scale, glad to have something to occupy his attention. *Seriously. Undone by a smile.* He'd thought himself too jaded for that.

Autumn walked ahead of him to the house. He placed his foot on the step gingerly, feeling it give a bit from his weight. She knocked on the screen door.

"Hi." A teenager in a baggy t-shirt and cut-off sweatpants swung the door open for them. She pushed a strand of hair from her forehead. "Sorry about how I look. I don't have anything else that fits comfortably. And I am *not* going to wear maternity clothes."

This was the new mother?

Autumn laughed. "Someone should have told you that."

"They did." She grimaced. "But I didn't believe them. I exercised and watched what I ate the whole pregnancy."

At second glance, the girl didn't look quite as young. He was just used to the 30- and 40-something professional woman he tended to see at his last practice.

"So, who's your friend?" The girl motioned to Jon.

Evidently, Autumn hadn't called ahead to tell her he was coming along.

"I'm sorry," Autumn said. "Megan, this is Dr. Hanlon from the Ticonderoga Birthing Center. He's interested in learning more about Kelly's and my home-birth practice."

The grin left Megan's face. Autumn should have cleared his coming with the mother. And he should have thought first before he'd decided to come. A free birther wouldn't welcome an obstetrician tagging along. And he couldn't stay without the mother's agreement.

"I don't have to stay if it makes you uncomfortable." Of course, he had no idea what he'd do for the two hours Autumn had said the visit would take.

A gusty wail sent Megan rushing from the room before she could respond, leaving Jon and Autumn in the middle of the room facing each other.

∽

AUTUMN SPOKE FIRST. "I should have called and cleared your coming with Megan." But she'd been too peeved at Kelly for suggesting she take Jon.

"Yes, you should have."

Autumn tensed. Even if she was in the wrong, he didn't have to agree so readily. She waited for him to lecture her on medical protocol as she'd heard him do more than once during their time at Samaritan.

"You can unclench your hands." He smiled the killer smile that she'd insisted to the other nurses at Samaritan had no effect on her. "What do you propose we do?" he asked.

Autumn relaxed her hands, warming at his acknowledgement that she was the person in control here. Except she wasn't in control, nor was her reaction to Kelly's suggestion Jon come on the visit very professional. "Let's leave it up to Megan. We should respect her wishes."

"Definitely," he agreed.

"There you go. All nice and dry," Megan crooned as she returned, patting her son on the bottom.

Autumn held out her hands and took the baby from his mother's arms. "Looking good," she said, holding the little boy so that Jon could see him.

Jon rocked back on his heels and nodded slightly in the direction of the baby.

She wasn't sure what that was about.

"Isn't he perfect?" the new mother asked looking from Autumn to Jon and back to her son.

Autumn drilled her gaze into Jon's. If he wanted to observe the visit, admiring the baby would be a good start in getting Megan to agree.

Jon cleared his throat. "He's a good-sized boy, and his color looks healthy."

Autumn resisted the inclination to roll her eyes at

Megan. "I apologize for not checking ahead to ask about bringing Dr. Hanlon."

"Jon," he said, turning his smile on the young mother.

Her expression softened. "That's okay." She turned to Jon. "You're just here to observe, right?"

That was it? One smile from Jon and Megan was fine with him being here? Autumn focused her attention on the infant in her arms, looking into his blue eyes as if he could give her an answer.

"That was the idea," Jon said, his tone light and, to Autumn's ears, flirtatious.

What's wrong with me? she silently asked the baby. Jon wasn't flirting and, if he was, why should she care? The infant scrunched his face as if he were going to cry. *Right.* It was Jon's attitude. She continued her unspoken conversation. The fact that he obviously thought his good looks were a balm to the situation. And that it seemed to be true.

"Is Dave going to join us?" Autumn asked.

"No, he got a call for work last night, framing a new camp on the lake." Megan hesitated. "We figured it was okay for him to go, since you'd be here this morning, and I'm sure Mom will stop by this afternoon on her way home from work."

Autumn caught Jon's thin-lipped expression before Megan did. He must not approve of Dave not being here. While it was nice to have someone to help with a newborn, from what she'd seen, Autumn was sure Megan would be fine by herself for the day.

"Dave does construction and lawn care during the summer," Megan said as if she had to explain. "We've had so much rain this year that he hasn't had a lot of work."

Autumn glared at Jon before turning to the new mother with a cheery, "Let's take a look at this guy. Can I use the changing table in the bedroom?" Autumn had used the beautiful maple table to examine the baby following his birth.

Megan gazed sideways at Jon. "Ah, the bed isn't made. We went back to sleep for a while after Dave left for work."

Autumn forced a laugh. "We're here to see you and the baby, not to check on your housekeeping. I'll wash up in your bathroom and meet you in the bedroom."

"Okay." Megan stepped toward the bedroom.

"Jon, can you bring the scale?" Autumn pointed to where they'd left it by the door when they'd come in.

"Yeah, sure."

Megan already had the baby on the changing table when Autumn joined her and Jon. She started undressing him. "This is a really cute onesie."

Megan beamed. "Yes, don't you love the little blue and yellow elephants? I bought it at the Hazardtown Community Church bargain shed. Mom said newborns outgrow things so fast, we should get as many things as we could there."

Autumn placed the baby in the sling of the scale Jon was holding ready. A frown marred his handsome face. "I know what you mean. Gram saved all of Aunt Jinx's clothes. She's only eight years older than I am. Dad didn't have to buy me anything new himself until I was ready for kindergarten."

"My sister gave me some things, too. But my nephew's hard on clothes, hard on everything."

"Do you want to record the weight?" Jon asked. "Seven pounds, fifteen ounces."

Autumn reached in the messenger bag slung over her shoulder for her iPad and came up empty. "I left my iPad at the office."

"I have some paper in the kitchen," Megan said.

"No need," Jon said. "My note pad is in my back pocket."

Autumn knew she had no reason to be irritated with Jon

being prepared, but she was, probably because she was unprepared.

He held the scale with one hand and reached around for the pad. "Here you go. Do you need a pen?"

"No, I have one."

"That's seven pounds, fifteen ounces," Jon repeated.

Autumn pressed the pen to the pad and wrote the baby's weight.

"You can check his birth weight when you get back to the office," Jon added.

Autumn wanted nothing better than to tell Jon the baby's birth weight, but she couldn't remember whether it was seven pounds, thirteen ounces or fourteen ounces. She was Megan's health care provider, not Jon. Well, Kelly was, actually, since she'd done the delivery. Autumn had assisted as the delivery nurse. A moment of darkness pressed on her. She could have done the delivery. Kelly had offered.

"He's gained two ounces since Saturday," Megan said.

The new mother's words put Autumn back on task. She finished her notation and picked up the baby. "Sounds like the nursing is going well." Autumn placed the baby on the changing table and examined him, noting his length and other vitals.

"No problems. He's eating about every three hours."

"Good. And the belly button is healing well." Autumn checked the baby's reflexes and redressed him. "You've made an appointment with your pediatrician?"

"With our family practitioner, Dr. Aikens, for a week from this coming Friday."

Jon's eyes narrowed. "Not a pediatrician?" he asked.

That was true to form. One thing Autumn had learned about him at Samaritan was that he favored using specialists, even if they weren't called for.

"Dr. Aikens is great with kids," Autumn said. "My step-mother and aunt both take their kids to her."

Jon was going to have to learn that practicing at the Ticonderoga center was going to be different than the suburban downstate practice he'd been with before coming here.

Autumn picked up the baby. "Let's go into the other room to talk. I want to go over a few things with you."

Autumn and Megan sat on the couch and Jon took the recliner across from them, leaning forward with his elbows resting on his knees. The baby started fussing rubbing his face back and forth on Autumn's shoulder. She patted his back.

"He may be hungry." Megan reached over and took him. "I guess not," she said when he showed no interest in eating but continued to fuss. "Maybe if I walk him. That's what Dave's been doing when he's fussy and doesn't want to eat or need a diaper change."

"I have a better idea," Autumn said. "Dr. Hanlon, would you do the honors?" She took the baby back from Megan, stood and walked him over to Jon. His eyes widened as she handed the infant to him.

"You could walk him outside. He really likes that. Here's his sunhat." Megan picked up a little blue hat from the table next to the couch and handed it to Autumn, who put it on the baby.

"All set," she said.

Jon rose from the chair slowly and walked gingerly to the door, as if he were afraid he was going to break the baby.

At the sound of the door closing behind him, Megan took her hand from her mouth and laughed. "I'm sorry, but it looks like he doesn't have much experience with babies."

"At least not after they're born," Autumn agreed. She went over the information she needed to cover with the new mother, conscious of Jon's frequent passes by the front door to check on their progress. "That covers everything. Walk out with me to relieve Dr. Hanlon."

Jon met them at the bottom of the porch steps. "I think he's asleep," he said, his voice low and gruff.

Megan reached up and took the baby from his shoulder.

"Either Kelly or I will be back on Wednesday about the same time," Autumn said.

"See you then." Megan went inside.

Jon helped her carry the equipment to the car and stash it in the back before opening her door for her. He climbed in the passenger side and turned to her.

She braced herself for his critique of the visit.

His blue eyes glowed. "I'm really impressed."

CHAPTER 5

*A*utumn sucked in a quick breath. She hadn't
expected *that.*

"But I have a few questions," he said.

She released the breath and pasted a smile on her face.
"Go ahead."

"Can I have my pad back?"

He was going to take notes? Her momentary euphoria
evaporated. She pulled the pad from her bag, tore off the
page she'd written the baby's vitals on and handed it to him.

Jon had his pen all ready. "Doesn't it bother you that she's
not taking the baby to a doctor for almost two weeks?"

"No. Kelly and I take responsibility for mother *and* baby
for the first two weeks. The whole family, actually."

"I see." His tone was quiet without the air of superiority
that sometimes crept in.

To collect herself before she responded, Autumn hit the
ignition. The engine purred to life. "It's part of what I trained
to do." She swallowed. The only thing she no longer felt
confident about was the main event—the birth—the core of
what made her a midwife.

"I don't have much experience with children, once they've been born, that is," Jon admitted.

She pressed the brake for the stop sign at the corner of Route 9. "I noticed."

"It was that obvious?"

Autumn laughed remembering the look on his face when she'd handed him the baby. "I'm afraid so. And you didn't seem all that comfortable with the kids at the camp lodge on Saturday. By the way, Anne apologizes for the way Sophie and Alex kept pestering you with questions until she laid down the law to them."

"It was okay, just different. My family isn't very close, and only one of us in my generation has had a child."

A shadow clouded his eyes, making him look vulnerable and less full of himself than he often did. She'd seen the same look of pain in his eyes last week when he was touring the center and she'd told him medical intervention wasn't needed with a normal birth.

"Kelly and I like to involve the whole family, including any siblings, in the pregnancy."

He dropped his gaze to the note pad and kept it there while he made a notation. He was hiding something. Something that Autumn suspected might make him a little less mechanical and more likeable.

"At the birth, too?"

"Yes." She waited for him to ask about keeping the birth area sanitary with all the family members there and was surprised when he didn't. "I can lend you some of my reference books if you want to read up on the protocol we follow." She and Kelly didn't call their routine a protocol, but Autumn figured it was a term Jon would relate to.

"Definitely. I'd like that."

The eager note in his voice warmed Autumn. After the way he'd seemed to be judging the situation at Megan's, she hadn't expected this interest in how she and Kelly worked.

He made another note on the pad and looked up. "Your holistic approach, does it include general education for the family?"

Autumn slowed for the left turn onto State Route 74. "I'm not sure I follow you."

"What to expect. The responsibilities and economics of being parents."

"I guess. Although I wouldn't have framed it in those words." As Hazard Cove Road and the Hazardtown Community Church came into sight on the left, Autumn checked the car clock. There was no way she'd make it to Ticonderoga to drop Jon off and back to pick up the twins by noon.

"Megan seems very young."

"She looks younger than she is. Megan is 22 and Dave's a little older. Not so young to be parents. Dad was 17 when I was born. A senior in high school."

Jon's surprised expression was exactly what she expected.

"Your mother?"

Autumn ignored the dull pain she always felt at any mention of the woman who'd abandoned her and Dad when Autumn was a few months old. "She was a sophomore in college."

That silenced him for a moment. "Because Megan is young, I wonder if she understands the priorities of being a parent, if that's part of your family education."

She couched her answer. "We talk about all kinds of things with our prospective parents. Remember, neither Kelly nor I had seen her before Saturday."

"It's just that those solar collectors on the house had to have been expensive. The money they spent on them might have been better spent on house repairs, like painting. Those peeling paint chips will be a danger when the baby is older. They may contain lead. And the steps need replacing, badly."

What made him think he was qualified to judge Megan and Dave? Autumn wanted to believe that his experience outside of his social strata was so limited that he didn't know better. But that was a stretch.

He cleared his throat. She went on before he could interrupt. "The solar water heater will save them money in the long run. And as Megan said, we've had a lot of rain. When the weather is good, Dave has to work long hours and doesn't have time to help her with home repairs like replacing the steps and painting the house. Believe me, they can't afford to pay someone to take care of things they could do themselves."

Jon folded his arms across his chest. "You can't argue that the changing table and cradle in the bedroom aren't an extravagance Megan and Dave apparently are ill-able to afford, that the money spent on handcrafted furniture couldn't have been used for better family purposes. I know what custom pieces like that go for downstate. I don't imagine they fetch much less up here, given the tourist trade."

As she came upon Hazardtown Community Church where the twin's childcare was, Autumn made a split-second decision. She flicked the directional and turned into the church parking lot. Hitting the break harder than necessary, she brought the car to a halt.

Jon raised an eyebrow.

She'd explain the stop after she answered his question. "Yes, I can argue with that. Megan's mother is a friend of Kelly's. She told me all about the pieces while Megan was in labor. The cradle is a family heirloom that Dave's grandfather made for Dave's father and his siblings. So that didn't cost them a dime. Dave's grandfather helped him make the changing table, so all that cost them was the wood." She paused and took a breath.

He opened his mouth as if to say something and then closed it.

"Can I give you a bit of advice? If you want to successfully direct the birthing center, which I assume is your goal, you need to realize that people here are different than you may be used to. The Adirondacks are not an affluent area by any stretch of the imagination. People here depend on family, and we make do with what we have. To answer your earlier question, yes. If I had a family that appeared to have its priorities, financial or otherwise, skewed away from the baby's best interests, I'd talk with the parents. That description doesn't fit Megan and Dave from what I know of their families and what I've seen of them."

"I see."

She hoped he did. Autumn fervently wanted the center to be successful to prevent the Adirondack Medical Center from having to close it or, maybe worse, sell it to JMH. Her gaze traced the rigid set of Jon's jaw. Of course, the plan could be for Jon to rescue the center for his grandfather to buy. But now wasn't the time to be thinking about that nor her precarious work situation, her soon-to-be-expired contract with Kelly or the possibility the center might close.

The sound of a car pulling up beside them drew her attention. Her aunt Jinx waved as she got out and Autumn rolled down her window.

"Hi, Autumn, Jon," Jinx said. "You here to pick up Sophie and Alex for swim lessons?" She tilted her head to the side so Autumn would block Jon's view of her and raised an eyebrow toward him.

"Sort of." Autumn glanced sidewise at Jon. "Jon came on a home visit with me, and I was on my way to take him back when I realized it's almost time for their swim lesson."

"Do you want me to take the twins to swim lessons with Izzy and Sam? I can bring them to you afterwards since I need to go into Ticonderoga and pick up some supplies for work this afternoon."

Autumn bit her lip. "That would work, but you might have two unhappy children on your hands. I don't have any appointments today and told the twins we'd spend the whole afternoon together."

Jinx waved her off. "It's only an hour or so. They'll get over it. Or, I have another idea. If you don't mind taking my kids down to Sunrise for swim lessons, I'll drive Jon to Ticonderoga, pick up my supplies and be back not too long after lessons are done." She looked at Jon.

"Works for me," he said.

Autumn hesitated. Jinx's offer was a good solution. But it left Jon with the last word in their conversation, which didn't sit well with her natural competitiveness. Not that she and Jon were in a competition. She didn't work for him, so it didn't matter if they had different ways of pursuing their mutual profession. "Your kids won't mind?" she asked.

"Not at all. I've been told more than once that you're much more fun than I am."

"All right. I'll stick around the camp until you get back. That's what the kids and I were going to do anyway."

"Sounds good. Ready, Jon?"

He kept his gaze on Autumn as he answered Jinx. "Ready. As much as I might enjoy an afternoon at the lake with Autumn and the kids, I should get back to my office."

She searched his words for a double meaning but didn't come up with one.

"I appreciate your taking me on the home visit," he said as he reached for the door handle. "I'll send you my notes in an email."

"O-kay."

He was going to write a report on this morning? She didn't know how else to respond to his statement. Or if it needed a response. Autumn climbed out of the car and watched Jinx pull away. As much as she tried to use his promise of his own home-visit report to refuel the irritation she'd felt toward him earlier, her thoughts kept coming back to his saying he would have liked to spend the afternoon at the beach with her and the kids. She stomped to the church hall where the daycare center was. What was with her? He'd only been making conversation with Jinx. Who wouldn't want to spend a beautiful day like today at the beach?

Jon closed the file on his computer. He was all caught up on the patient records for the center and ready to start his expectant mother appointments tomorrow. Not that it looked like a very busy schedule. Nothing like the downstate practice he'd been with prior to coming here. Some days, he'd felt like he was on an assembly line. He'd had so little time on each case. Autumn and Kelly's approach to patient time struck him as a good safety net to help pinpoint potential problems with a pregnancy and address them before delivery. His thoughts went to how he could integrate their approach in his practice. Coupling it with technology could improve outcomes.

Jon opened his report on the home visit and added that observation. Leaning back in his chair, he skimmed what he'd written and contemplated whether to add a comment about Autumn's baby scale. To him, it had looked a lot like a high-end digital sports fishing scale. He leaned his elbow into the padded arm of his chair and rested his head against his thumb and forefinger. He wondered how the accuracy compared to the digital scale he had in his office. He straightened. Rather than say anything in the report, he'd do some research and share the results with her. Surely she'd be interested. The thought warmed him. He'd benefited from their time together this morning. Why not reciprocate?

The sharp ring of his desk phone jerked him from his thoughts. He spun the chair around and picked up the receiver. "Dr. Hanlon."

"Jay, it's Grandfather."

As if he wouldn't recognize his voice.

"I can't make our dinner at the Sagamore. There's a facility in Broome County that I want to check out. Acquisitions sent me a report yesterday."

On Sunday? He didn't know why he was surprised.

"The facility is still struggling to recover from the flooding there last year. We'd be able to pick it up for much less than it's worth."

Jon bit his tongue and offered a silent prayer for help to stop himself from telling Grandfather what he thought of his business practices. He knew his words would fall on deaf ears. Grandfather didn't care.

"JMH has to strike while the iron is hot if we're going to best Unified Health Care," his grandfather said. "Did you read their last quarterly report? They're gaining on us in acquisitions in the Northeast."

Jon couldn't stop the longing triggered by his grandfather's use of "us" as if Jon were part of the family business, as if they shared more than a set of familial genes. "No, I haven't."

"You should. I'll e-mail you a copy."

Jon ignored his grandfather's offer. "Will Nana still be coming?" He'd been looking forward to seeing her. They could have a nice dinner together without Grandfather.

"I told her that you're too far out of the way now. I'll be

coming back through Binghamton, not Albany. And she's not happy. But business is business. You understand."

What Jon understood was that he wasn't worth his grandfather's time and Nana's feelings weren't worth his consideration. He swallowed the bile that rose to his throat.

"I'll give Nana a call. Maybe invite her to come and visit here for a few days. She could take the Amtrak Adirondack train."

"Sure, you do that." His grandfather clicked off without saying goodbye.

Jon dropped the phone receiver into the cradle and struggled to contain his anger. This was the man who used to lecture him as a kid on good manners, proper behavior, and consideration of others? Jon grasped the edge of the desk, squeezed hard and released his grip to tap down his anger. *Guess Grandfather's lessons don't apply when business is involved.*

When it came to his family, finding any warm feelings could be extremely hard. Except for Nana and Brad. He'd enjoy having Nana come for a few days over a weekend so he could spend time with her. He picked up his cell phone and pressed her contact picture. As the phone rang, he pictured Nana and him having coffee on the patio at the duplex—with Autumn. Nana would like Autumn. His chest tightened against the hollow that opened in it. A hollow that he had no rational explanation for and no idea how to fill.

"Autumn, rate my splash," her seven-year-old cousin, Isabella, shouted. She did a cannonball off the family dock located up the beach from the camp's aquatics area.

"Me, too. Me, too," Autumn's twin siblings said as they copied Isabella.

Autumn's aunt Jinx plopped down beside her on the blanket she'd spread on the stony beach. "It's not enough that she's the oldest and the biggest, she also has to come up with challenges she has to know she'll win."

"I wonder where she gets that from," Autumn said. "Wait, I have this aunt that used to often set me up for—"

"Stop. That was learned behavior from your father. And I have a niece of mine who tends to do only those things she's best at."

A pall rolled over Autumn. Was that why she'd stopped delivering babies? Because she wasn't perfect at it? She put her hand to her forehead as much to hide her expression as to shield the sun as she watched the kids do another round of jumps. "Guilty as charged. I'm a Hazard."

Jinx laughed. "Something we all have to live with." She followed Autumn's gaze to the dock. "Where's Ian?"

"At the library. There's some program this week where kids can write and produce their own books. He's going to a friend's afterwards."

"Funny how much he's like Anne. You wouldn't have caught my brother inside on a day like this when he was Ian's age, and he would have considered inside at the library a punishment."

"Dad would still see the library as a punishment on a beautiful day like this."

"I think it's interesting how many of Anne's and Neal's traits Ian has picked up. But he was only two when her friends were killed, and she and Neal adopted him."

Autumn nodded. Anne and Dad had both readily accepted Ian as their own. "While we're on the subject of family, what do you think of Grandpa's idea of giving Gram a surprise birthday party?"

"Not like him at all. Anne must be behind it. She really

soaks up all the family stuff. But who can blame her? Her family is so cold and distant."

Like Jon's, from what Autumn could tell. "Yes, the e-mail invitations were totally Anne, right down to my 'and guest.'"

"Isabella, give the inner tube to Sam," Jinx shouted. "It's his turn." She turned back to Autumn. "Do you have someone in mind? Dr. Dreamy, by any chance?"

Autumn's heartbeat quickened. "Not you, too?"

Jinx wrinkled her nose. "What do you mean?"

"The Dr. Jonathan Mitchell Hanlon fan club. He smiles and women swoon for miles around."

"You have to admit that he's easy to look at. You're not interested, even a little?"

"There's got to be more to a man than looks."

"Right, like important things in common. You deliver babies. He delivers babies. So you're both used to crazy work schedules."

Except she didn't deliver babies anymore, and she had a strong feeling Jon wouldn't understand why not.

"Admit it," Jinx said. "There's a spark. I saw it Saturday and again this afternoon in the church parking lot."

Autumn wanted to give her aunt a flat-out "no, there's nothing between us," except she didn't lie. And while maybe not a spark, she did feel some connection to Jon. "We're colleagues, possibly working on being friends. That's all there is."

"Come on," her aunt prodded.

Autumn flicked a pebble off the blanket. "When we worked together at Samaritan, Jon had a reputation as a player. He dated my roommate, Kate, and dumped her for no apparent reason. Broke her heart. She really liked him."

"That's the Kate you used to refer to as the drama queen?"

"Yes." Kate had been high strung. "But she seemed truly

hurt, and Jon wasted no time after the breakup before asking me out. When I said no, he moved on to another nurse. His actions upheld his reputation."

"People change," Jinx said, "and there are usually two sides to every story."

Autumn stared out at the lake. Her aunt was right, but she'd need some definite sign Jon had changed before she could even think about the possibility of them ever being anything more than friends.

CHAPTER 6

*Y*esterday's warm sunshine had been replaced by a chilly downpour. Autumn opened the door to the birthing center and tapped her umbrella on the entry way rug before closing it. A flirty laugh drew her attention to the front desk, where Jon was lounging against the wall talking with the receptionist and a woman Autumn didn't recognize. The woman gazed up at him with a look Autumn had seen all too often at Samaritan.

She clenched the umbrella and ducked down the hall to her office. Jon had e-mailed her his report on yesterday's home visit, and she wasn't ready to talk about it, not until she'd had time to give it a good read. She hadn't been able to resist opening the report and skimming it at home. It had seemed surprisingly complimentary, considering the direction their conversation had been going when Jinx had interrupted them.

She opened the door to the office and Kelly swooped down on her like an eagle on its prey.

"I'm glad you're here early. I have a few things I want to

go over with you before Kari and I head over to the Donnellys'," Kelly said. "Rachel's in labor."

Autumn liked Kelly well enough, aside from her propensity to be a workaholic and a little too in charge at times. But Autumn couldn't help wishing Kelly had already left. She'd given herself just enough time this morning to read Jon's report, in case she ran into him later, and tackle some of the office work that was piling up again before her first appointment.

Autumn hitched her bag up on her shoulder. "What's up?"

"I've hired an office assistant."

"When?"

"Yesterday, after you'd left for the day."

Just like that? Kelly had hired someone without even consulting her? Autumn shifted her weight. She knew Kelly was getting impatient with her not taking on any new deliveries. Maybe this was her way of telling her she wasn't pulling her weight.

"I thought we were going to interview Kari's cousin Lexi for the job."

"I did. Kari gave me her resume, and I interviewed her by phone."

"Oh." Kelly's explanation didn't make her feel any better. "When does she start?"

"That's the best part," Kelly said with a grin. "She already has. I told her how desperate we were, and she drove to Kari's from Syracuse last night and reported for work this morning. Kari and Eli are going to help her finish clearing out her apartment in Syracuse this weekend."

"She knows the job is only temporary?"

"Yeah. Her lease is up, and she was going to come and visit Kari either way."

"I should go introduce myself. Are they in the back?"

"No, Kari took her around to meet the other staff."

Lexi was the woman at the front desk making cow eyes at Jon. Autumn shook off the ridiculous stab of jealousy. "I think I saw her at the front desk when I came in. A tall, willowy brunette?" Who, now that she thought about it, looked a lot like her former roommate, Kate.

"That's her."

"I didn't see Kari, though."

Kelly shrugged. "They'll be back in a minute, and I'll introduce you. While we wait, I need to talk with you about Lisa Kent. I've decided to admit her to the center and induce labor. She's a week and a half overdue and was two centimeters dilated when she came in for her appointment yesterday. I'd like you to admit her, induce labor and keep an eye on her progress."

A chill ran through Autumn. Kelly was leaving her with a mother who would be in labor.

Kelly pursed her lips. "No need to look like a deer caught in headlights. The baby probably won't make her appearance until sometime tomorrow. And, if she does, I have Jon on call."

Lovely. Kelly was losing patience with her for not carrying her weight with the maternity part of the practice and, if Lisa had her baby, Jon probably would be full of questions as to why she wasn't doing the birth. Questions she wasn't ready to answer for him, that she didn't even have answers to. She should be past the trauma of Suzy's complications.

"Sure. I plan on being here all day. I have some appointments this morning and was going to catch up on paperwork this afternoon to fill the time until my four o'clock appointment. What time did you tell Lisa to come?"

"Ten thirty. I saw that you had a break in appointments then."

"That'll work." She pushed a strand of hair that had come

loose from her French braid behind her ear. "Have you talked with Jon?"

"Yes. I said we have a mother coming in for an induction and that Kari and I are heading out for a home delivery."

"He didn't ask why I wasn't covering for you?"

"No, and I didn't tell him about your problem, if that's your concern."

It wasn't a problem. It was a very real fear. But Kelly could think whatever she wanted.

"He seemed pleased that I asked. Since Dr. Ostertag didn't take on new patients in his last months here, Jon doesn't have many mothers who are due anytime soon."

"Jon likes deliveries. I remember that from Samaritan. Some of the other residents did nothing but complain about being on call, especially the ones who planned to specialize in GYN surgery. Not Jon. He relished it. I think he'd have loved it if that was all he had to do."

"How's that?"

"He wasn't comfortable dealing with the fathers and other family members. Or, for that matter, with the mothers. But at least with the women he could get by with his good looks and heart-melting smile."

Kelly raised her eyebrows.

Autumn wasn't sure if it was out of curiosity or her poor choice of words. Jon's smile didn't melt her heart, just seemingly every other woman's. "I think that in his perfect world someone else would handle all the prenatal and post-natal contact. All he'd have to do was make his appearance for the birth."

"Interesting. No bedside manner?"

Autumn thought back to the home visit yesterday. She was being a little harsh. "It's not that he doesn't want to relate to people, it's more like he can't." She shook her head. "His care is textbook perfect, but mechanical. Birth as a medical procedure that has to be executed perfectly." She bit her tongue as she remembered what Jinx had said yesterday about her not doing anything she couldn't do well.

"Hmmm." Kelly pressed her forefinger to her lips. "If Lisa's baby does come, you'd better assist at the delivery. She needed a lot of encouragement and handholding with the last one. Her labor was pretty intense. He came so fast."

"How fast?"

"A few hours after her water broke."

"Are you setting me up?"

"What do you mean?" Kelly asked all innocent.

Autumn tapped her umbrella on the floor. "You said you didn't expect the baby to come until tomorrow."

"In most cases, she wouldn't."

"But in this case, she likely will."

"Maybe." Kelly huffed. "Okay. We have to work with Jon. A routine birth like Lisa's is a good opportunity to establish a working relationship, in case one of our mothers develops prenatal complications and we have to refer her to Jon for care. You know him already. You can scope him out for us."

Autumn relaxed.

"And, if you assist, we'll get paid for at least part of the delivery."

Autumn's temper flared. "If you think I'm not doing my part, just say so."

"Sorry. I didn't mean to sound like that. I'm a little tense about Stephanie going away to college this fall and the looming tuition payment."

Kelly's apology didn't ring entirely true. Autumn knew what the practice brought in and that Kelly's parents had set up a substantial education fund for their only granddaughter.

"That's okay," she ground out. "One of the things I'm going to do this afternoon is add another birth and breastfeeding class to the center's education schedule." Autumn bit her lip. She didn't need to tell Kelly that as if she were validating her value to the practice.

"Good. You can explain to Lexi how to contact Marketing at the medical center to get them on the schedule and publicized."

Was that another dig?

"And here she is," Kelly said as the office door swung open to let Kari and Lexi in. "Lexi Zarinski. Autumn Hazard, the other third of Ticonderoga Midwifery's staff."

"Hi. Kari and the kids have told me all about you. I feel like I know you already."

"Has she also told you how glad we are you're here? We are getting buried in paperwork." *Most of which I've been doing with little recognition of my effort from Kelly.*

"So I've heard. Kari has me set to catch up on the filing this morning."

"Great. I'll be in my office getting ready for appointments. Just give me a shout if you need anything."

"Will do."

Autumn glanced from Kari to Kelly. "I'll see you guys later, or tomorrow, depending on how things go." She waited to see if Kelly was going to direct her to check in with her on Lisa.

"I'll give you a call later if I can," Kelly said.

Yep, to check up on her. Autumn dragged her feet to her office, mulling over what Kelly might have meant by "the other third" of the staff. Was she just making conversation or was she relegating her to delivery nurse status with Kari and Kristen?

∼

"HELLO AGAIN."

Lexi looked up from her computer. "Dr. Hanlon."

"Jon," he automatically corrected her.

"Jon," she repeated.

"Autumn wasn't with Mrs. Kent in the birthing suite. Is she here in her office?"

"Yes. She stopped back because she had an appointment scheduled. Do you want me to get her?"

"Autumn's with the patient?"

"No, she's alone. She caught the woman scheduled before she'd left home and rescheduled the appointment." Lexi started to rise from her seat.

"Don't get up. I'll go back." He didn't know what it was about Lexi. He didn't know her, but there was something off-putting about the woman.

He knocked on Autumn's half-closed door.

"Come on in, Lexi. We're not formal around here."

"I'm not Lexi."

Autumn started. "Jon."

"Hi. Lexi told me you were done with your appointments for the day. I am, too, and I thought we should go check on Mrs. Kent's progress."

Autumn wrinkled her forehead. "Oh, you mean Lisa. As I said, we're not formal here."

He hadn't noted the patient's first name when he'd brought up the computer records to familiarize himself with the case. "Kelly had said you were going to break Mrs. Kent's —Lisa's—water to induce labor, but I saw you didn't."

"Lisa went into labor on her own early this morning, so I decided not to. The less interference, the better."

Jon nodded. "Of course." He wasn't in the habit of inducing labor, either, unless medically necessary.

Autumn's desk phone buzzed, wiping the surprised look off her face.

"Excuse me." She turned sideways to take the call, and he

studied the way her hair crisscrossed down the back of her head into a long braid falling down her back. He definitely preferred her hair long to the spikey way she'd had it at Samaritan.

She hung up. "You're timing is perfect. That was Kristen, our other delivery nurse. Lisa is seven centimeters dilated. We're going to have a baby."

Her words shot through him like a jolt of electricity jump starting a car battery and he recalled the awe and joy on Autumn's face during the births they'd done together at Samaritan. When she'd said she was concentrating on other aspects of the practice, rather than delivering babies, he'd thought that delight must have worn off for her. But her wide grin said his assumption was off base.

"Let's go!" Autumn's enthusiasm fueled his. He matched his stride to hers as they walked down the hall toward the birthing suites.

Autumn knocked on the closed door and a man opened it. "Hi, Greg," she said. "We met at the expectant parents night."

"Right." He rubbed his hand over his closely cropped hair and gazed at the mother-to-be, who gripped the windowsill as a contraction rippled through her. He winced. "You'd think this would be easier the second time around."

"How are you doing, Lisa?" Autumn asked.

"Okay. I'm better standing. But I'm starting to feel like I should push."

"Great. That's probably pressure from your water wanting to break. But we'll wash up just in case your baby decides to follow. This is Dr. Hanlon." Autumn introduced him. "Lisa and Greg Kent."

Jon extended his hand to Greg and then Lisa. In the slight lull that followed, he thought about telling them to call him Jon.

"Kelly told you he'd be doing the delivery?"

Lisa nodded between breaths as another contraction started.

"He's new here, and we want to break him in right."

Jon stiffened. He'd certainly delivered as many babies as she had. Probably more.

Greg rolled his eyes. "Women," he said with an exaggerated sigh. "I suppose this is their domain."

Jon agreed to a point. But he was as capable of delivering a baby as any woman.

Lisa squeezed her husband's hand hard. "I'd be perfectly happy to have you take on this part next time, not that there's going to be a next time."

"That's not what you were saying a few weeks ago."

"It's what I'm saying now." Lisa groaned in pain.

Jon hated when the parents got into it in the delivery room. He'd had births where he'd wanted to ask the father to leave to reduce the tension for the good of the mother and the baby. He hadn't though.

"Hey, you two. You can discuss family planning another time," Autumn said. "We've got work to do here. Hop on the bed so we can take a look. Dr. Hanlon, would you like to do the honors?"

Jon caught Lisa silently mouthing "I love you" to Greg. Her husband mouthed "me, too" back.

Feeling like an intruder on their intimacy, Jon looked at Autumn, who was smiling at the couple. She was so at ease with them. He reached for his pad to make a note to himself about his observations and stopped. He wasn't an observer this time. The whoosh of Lisa's water breaking snapped his attention back to her.

He jumped back, hands up, conscious that Autumn was close behind him. He wasn't any more comfortable having someone looking over his shoulder now than he'd been in medical college. But he'd tolerated it as part of the learning process.

"Looking good," she said. "Kelly was right when she said that once you get started you don't waste any time. The head is crowning."

"Hey, that was my line," Jon said.

Autumn stepped to his left and replaced the wet pads on the bed with dry ones. She and Greg exchanged another look, making him feel superfluous.

If she'd wanted to do the delivery, she could have. She still could, except Lisa was Kelly's patient, and Kelly had asked him to do the delivery. It wasn't his place to speculate why. He studied the placement of the baby's head and checked the instrument tray at his right, although he knew everything was there. He'd supervised the preparation of the room himself before the Kents had arrived.

He glanced to his right. Autumn had moved away and was talking with the nurse, who was preparing the warm towels for the baby. He couldn't imagine Kelly not trusting Autumn's competence. He'd seen Autumn in action at Samaritan. He'd had colleagues who'd given up obstetrics, but generally for the more lucrative gynecological surgery.

"How are we doing?" she called over.

He wasn't sure if she was talking to him or the parents. "About to start second stage."

"Is that right, Lisa?" Autumn asked. "Do you feel like pushing?"

"Yes," the mother-to-be grunted. "I said that before."

"Then we should be welcoming Ingrid very soon."

She knew the baby's name, and he'd vacillated about telling the parents to call him Jon. From what he'd seen of the Paradox Lake/Ticonderoga area, Autumn and Kelly probably knew all of Greg and Lisa's family members, too. The only one of his deliveries where he'd gotten to know the parents was a couple whom he'd already known from his condo building.

Greg's "her hair looks red, Lis" as he looked at the mirror behind Jon brought him back into focus on the birth. His neck grew hot. Something could have happened while he was letting his thoughts drift. He reached down and caught the baby as she made her appearance with a loud squall. Jon held her for a moment before placing her on Lisa's chest.

"Here's your new daughter."

She was pink and perfect as far as his quick assessment could tell. A rush of joy flowed through him. He clamped the umbilical cord and reached for another clamp.

"Can you hand Greg the cord scissors?"

Jon looked at Autumn and blinked.

"So he can cut the cord."

"Of course." He should have asked, rather than thinking to do it himself. Fathers and other birth partners routinely cut the cord. He handed Greg the scissors.

Once they had the family all settled, Jon and Autumn stepped into the other room to give Lisa and Greg some privacy.

"That went well," Jon said.

"It did. Lisa and Greg are a cute couple. You should see their little boy. He's a miniature Greg." Autumn swung her arms forward and then stretched them back. "I'm always so jazzed after a birth."

"Me, too. I often go running."

"I'm not that ambitious. But you may notice that the only time my house is really clean is after a birth."

The joy he and Autumn had shared bringing little Ingrid into the world still shone on Autumn's face. "I'm a little puzzled as to why Kelly asked me to cover today. You would have been fine without me."

She stilled. "Because I don't do births anymore."

The vehemence in her voice puzzled him even more. Why wasn't she doing births when she so obviously enjoyed them? Not that he was going to ask right now. His intended compliment had snuffed out the warm afterglow of the wonder they'd just experienced together.

She looked at her watch. "I should check on Lisa and the baby."

"Yes, we should."

"You don't have to. I can handle things. Go take your run. Seriously. The time with the new parents afterwards is one of my favorite parts of a birth."

He hesitated. Lisa was Kelly and Autumn's patient. He'd done his part, needed or not. He didn't have to stay. "I could stand to burn off some energy and the sticky buns my nurse brought into the office this morning." It couldn't hurt to try to tease back some of the joy they'd shared in the birthing room.

"And I should be right behind you working off the half a carrot cake my grandmother dropped off yesterday because she knows it's my favorite." Her voice was lighter.

"I can stay and give you a hand here. Then you could join me in my run."

Autumn burst into laughter. Tears streamed down her face, and she bent over and hugged herself.

"What's so funny?"

"I—" She choked to get control of her laughter. "Sorry. A little excess energy on my part, there. I've seen you take off for your lake run. And return. I'm afraid you'd lose me before the end of the driveway. I'm more of a hiker or a leisurely stroll around the lake type of person."

Autumn had noticed him taking his runs? He stood straight, his shoulders back. "Yeah?" He grinned and reached over to wipe a tear off her cheek.

She leaned into his touch, tilting her face up to him.

He locked his gaze with hers as he lowered his lips. The kiss was soft, sweet, and short.

Greg peered around the doorway from the birth room. "Autumn, we have a question."

She spun away from him so fast, her braid flew out and hit him. "I'll be right there." Greg disappeared into the other room, and Autumn turned back to Jon.

"I...I," he stuttered like a teenage boy caught by a father stealing a kiss from his daughter.

"It's okay," she said. "It's the adrenalin overload. I'm sure it's not the first time you've been caught up in the wonder of birth and reacted instinctively to share your exuberance."

Was that some kind of dig? The pounding in his chest slowed. He knew he'd gained a reputation at Samaritan that wasn't entirely undeserved. He liked women and had dated a lot of them. But he wasn't in the habit of kissing his delivery staff no matter how exhilarating the birth.

"Have a good run." She waved him off.

That was it? She hadn't felt any attraction at all from adrenalin or otherwise? He'd been attracted to Autumn at Samaritan and still was, even though the timing was as wrong now as it had been then.

Forty minutes later, Jon was in his jogging shorts and muscle shirt racing up Hazard Cove Road making what might be his best time yet around the lake. As he hit the beach path, he looked out across the placid blue waters and speculated whether his speed was triggered by the lingering adrenalin rush or because he wanted to get back home to check in with Autumn to see how she and Lisa and Ingrid were doing. Before he'd given into the impulse to kiss Autumn, he'd meant to tell her that he wanted to go with her to Lisa's follow-up home visit.

His feet pounded the path, throwing small pebbles behind him. Sharing the birth today with Autumn had made him more curious to know what had caused her to give up catching babies. It had to be major, and he probably wouldn't find out until she was ready to tell him. If they ever got that close. But he wasn't here to get close to Autumn, or anyone else. He breathed deeply and exhaled, thinking of their kiss. As inviting as that might be.

CHAPTER 7

*A*utumn juggled her bag and the box of trivia paraphernalia. Somehow, she'd ended up taking it home again after their last meet. She wiped her hand on her jeans and pushed open the door to the Old Ireland Pub. Attendance at the trivia nights had dropped off steadily lately, following the spiraling trajectory of her social life in general.

The sound of a vehicle entering the church parking lot made her turn. She knit her brows in concern when she recognized Kari's SUV. Kari had said she wasn't coming because she was the on-call delivery nurse tonight. Autumn checked her cellphone to see if Kelly had tried to contact her. If they had a birth and she hadn't been able to get through, Kelly might have sent Kari to track her down here. *No bars.* Autumn's heart dropped. Three of their mothers-to-be were overdue. If they'd all gone into labor, Kelly would have only Jon—Autumn swallowed the lump that clogged her throat— and her to help cover. The other center midwife was on vacation this week.

Kari pulled the van parallel to the sidewalk and the

passenger side door opened. "Hey, Autumn. I'm early," Lexi called. "My car died on the way home from work today, so I had to hitch a ride with Kari. She's on her way to a birth."

Autumn let the door close and walked to the van. "Hi. I'm glad you came." She looked past Lexi to Kari. "Who's having the baby? Tanya, Sara or Allie?"

"None of the above," Kari said. "It's one of Maureen's mothers."

Autumn shoved her hand in her front pocket. She hadn't considered that Maureen, the other midwife they covered births for, might have any of her mothers giving birth this week.

"She's two weeks early. I'm meeting Kelly at the center."

Autumn nodded. "I'll talk to you tomorrow."

"Unless we need to call you in. Tanya, Sara and Allie." Kari laughed as she repeated the names of their three overdue mothers. "We know where to find you."

Autumn swallowed. She hoped they wouldn't have to.

"And Jon if you need him," Lexi added. "He told me he was coming tonight." She closed the SUV door behind her, and Kari drove away.

Lexi reopened the pub door for Autumn.

"It looks like there won't be many of us tonight," Autumn said.

Lexi smiled. "I don't mind a small group."

No, Autumn didn't suppose Lexi would, as long as Jon showed. She'd been full of questions about Jon today after she'd learned that Autumn had worked with him before. Autumn chided herself for being petty. She was transferring her stress about the possibility of being called to a birth to Lexi. What did it matter to her if Lexi was interested in Jon? She was his type. A tall, willowy brunette, like her former roommate, Kate.

"Let's grab a few tables," Autumn said.

"Sure."

As the two women formed a square of four small tables, another voice greeted them.

"Hi. By the looks of things, I guess I'm not as late as I thought I was."

Autumn turned to see Becca Norton, a friend of her aunt Jinx's who taught history at the high school.

"Not late at all. Come on in. I wasn't sure if you were coming. Did anyone else mention coming?" Autumn asked. "I didn't get much of a response from my reminder text."

Becca shook her head. "Not that I remember, except Jon. He told me Sunday afternoon at the lake when he was teaching Brendon how to fish."

Jon and Becca? How did Becca know Jon well enough that he was teaching her son to fish? Unwarranted jealousy squeezed her heart and bolstered her resolve not to give into Jon's appeal.

"But that doesn't mean more people aren't coming," Becca quickly added.

The slight sense of defeat that had pressed Autumn when she'd arrived intensified. It looked like the group tonight would be her and Jon, if he came, and his latest fan following.

"Excuse me." A tall blond man who looked familiar to Autumn poked his head in the lounge. "I'm looking for the trivia match."

"Yes, I'm Autumn Hazard."

"Josh Donnelly."

"Mrs. Donnelly's—I mean Stowe's—grandson?" The elderly retired teacher had remarried a couple of years ago, but Autumn still thought of her as Mrs. Donnelly. "You were a couple of years ahead of me at school. I thought you looked familiar." Autumn realized she hadn't introduced Lexi to

Becca. "This is Lexi Zarinski. She's new to the area. And Becca Norton."

"Hi." Josh's eyes lingered on Lexi. "In a way, I'm new, too. I recently moved back to Paradox Lake to take a job with GreenSpaces."

Autumn's spirits lightened. As she'd told Kari, the group could use some new men. She checked the clock. It wasn't seven o'clock yet. Others, besides Jon, might still show up.

"And I know Mrs. Norton," Josh said.

"Becca, please. You're making me feel old. I had Josh in my class the first year I taught at Schroon Lake Central."

Autumn heard another muffled male voice in the hall and her pulse ticked up. Jon?

"Hi, everyone." Tessa Hamilton walked in, followed by Jon. "I've brought a new member."

He'd come with Tessa? Another conquest she didn't know about? But he always had been a fast worker. What was with her? Since Lexi had said Jon planned to come to Singles Group, her every second thought had been about him and critical of him. So they'd kissed. She had to put it out of her mind as he'd obviously done.

Jon smiled, and all of the women smiled back.

"I ran into Jon at General Store on my way over here," Tessa said. "We discovered the clerk had mixed up our orders when we got in our cars, and after we exchanged them, introduced ourselves, and found we were both headed here, we decided to eat together at the outdoor picnic table. Her gaze softened.

Tessa, too? What about Becca? That was last weekend, though, and the Jon she'd known at Samaritan hadn't been known for long-term relationships. But unlike Lexi, who'd pressed her lips into a tight line, Becca didn't look at all put out that he'd had supper with Tessa. Autumn pushed a nonexistent stray hair behind her ear. What did any of it matter if there was anything to matter? It wasn't as if she were interested in Jon.

Jon turned to Josh. "I don't think we've met. I'm Jon Hanlon."

Josh shook Jon's extended hand and introduced himself.

"Should we sit down and get started? I think this may be all of us for tonight." Autumn unpacked the game stuff on the table in front of her and smiled when she saw Josh quickly slip in next to Lexi at another table. Jon sat in the chair at Autumn's right.

JON WATCHED Autumn as she distributed the game cards. He hadn't known that she was the group leader. Not that it would have made any difference in his coming. He rather liked the idea. It would let him see another facet of her, a personal side, that could help in their professional relationship. Now that he'd had time to analyze the Kent birth, he realized what a mistake it had been to give into the urge to kiss Autumn. He wasn't ready to give the long-term commitment to her or the Paradox Lake area he was sure she would want. Keeping their relationship strictly professional was the only way to go. To fuel his determination, he'd told himself a midwife was almost an obstetrician, and he didn't date other doctors.

She looked around when she finished. "As some of you know, this is kind of a reorganization meeting. We took a month off. So, along with what may be a quick match since there are so few of us, I thought we might talk about the group, getting it going again. While the matches aren't limited to single people, we are the closest thing to a singles group Paradox Lake has."

The group looked around at each other.

"I have an idea," Jon said. "The trivia matches are bi-weekly, right?" He didn't wait for an answer. "We could do Sunday afternoon movies or see some of the local attractions together on alternate weeks. I'd like to get to know the area better, although you guys may have seen everything already."

"I haven't," Lexi said with a broad smile.

Jon tapped his foot. He wished he could put his finger on what it was about the woman that grated on him so. Lexi twirled a strand of her dark hair. *That was it.* Lexi looked a lot like Autumn's former roommate.

"How would we work the movies?" Becca asked. "Private screening at the XX, maybe after the usual Sunday matinee?" She looked at Tessa.

Tessa had told him how she'd recently inherited the theater in Schroon Lake from her grandfather.

"No can do," Tessa said. "Even though I technically could show DVDs people may have, I can't. Copyright infringement. I'd have to rent the episodes from my distributor, and that could cost us a couple of hundred dollars each."

"Oh, well," Becca said. "I thought it would be great for me if I could bring my kids, so I wouldn't have to ask my ex-mother-in-law to babysit. I'm not sure I'd want to inflict them on someone's home."

"We could start with a movie at my place, first." Jon said. "It's okay with me if you bring Brendon and Ari. They're good kids." Or at least they had been the afternoon he'd spent at the lake with them, teaching Brendon how to fish. He'd run into the family when he'd walked down to the Camp Sunrise dock to check out the lake fishing. The boy had chatted him up about fishing, saying he wanted to go to a fishing derby with Autumn's brother, Ian. The gist he'd gotten was that Brendon's father had said he come and take the boy fishing, then cancelled. Becca had mentioned she didn't know any more about fishing than Brendon did. So he'd agreed to give the boy some tips.

Jon waited for Autumn's mouth to drop open in surprise at his statement about Becca's kids. As he'd told her, it wasn't that he didn't like kids. He just wasn't used to them. The hours with Brendon had been easy. Jon liked to fish, and the boy was an avid student, although it had made Jon somewhat uncomfortable that Brendon's main purpose in learning to fish had been to beat his friend at the derby. A goal that it sounded like Ian shared.

He didn't know why people had to turn everything into a competition. It certainly hadn't benefitted his family life.

"That's nice of you," Becca said.

"Becca, if you don't want to ask your ex-mother-in-law, you probably could leave the kids with Dad and Anne," Autumn said. "Brendon could hang out with Ian and the twins could entertain Ari. Or I'm sure Gram wouldn't mind watching them."

Send the kids somewhere else. There was the contradiction Jon had expected earlier. While, truth be told, he was all for keeping the group get togethers adult, Autumn was presumptuous to offer her family's services without asking them first. He'd learned his lesson young not to ask for or expect anything from his family unless he was prepared to give twice as much back in return.

"I'd hate to impose on them," Becca said. "I'm sure I can work out some arrangement."

Everyone looked at Autumn. She bit her bottom lip and released it. She couldn't possibly disagree when the rest of the group was all on board. And she did want to get the group active again.

"Sounds like a go to me," she said. "Next Sunday afternoon at Jon's. He can give me the details and I'll text everyone a reminder. Now. Let's drinks some drinks and get this game going."

After they finished with Tessa and Becca the winners, Lexi checked her phone and announced, "I need to catch a ride back to Kari's with someone, if I can." She looked directly at Jon and smiled. "Eli was going to pick me up, but his American Legion meeting in Ticonderoga is running late. My car's in the garage."

A clap of thunder rattled the pub windows before anyone could offer, and the ping of raindrops sounded on the slate roof.

"That leaves me out," Jon said, ignoring the relief he felt at having a good reason for not offering. "I rode my bike tonight."

"I'll give you a lift, Lexi," Josh said.

"Thanks," she said, her smile for Josh a little less bright. Or so it seemed to Jon.

"You, too, Jon, if you need one."

"I'm good. I'm just up Hazard Cove Road."

"He's renting the other half of Dad's duplex," Autumn added, placing her hand on her hip with a satisfied smile he couldn't decipher. It was almost as if she were staking a claim on him. *Right, Hanlon, only in your dreams.* He stilled. All of the women were appealing, but Autumn was the only one he was attracted to.

"All right," Josh said, smiling at Lexi and bringing Jon out of his thought. "Then it's just you and me, Lexi."

Jon caught the definite gleam of interest in the other man's eyes and silently wished him well.

Everyone else but Autumn left. She gathered the trivia stuff. "Do you want a ride home? Your bike will be fine here for the night."

"No, thanks. It's not that far. I'll be fine."

"You're sure?"

He silently preened at her casual concern. "I'm sure."

"I'll follow you home." She crossed the room to the door.

He didn't need anyone to follow him but liked the idea of Autumn wanting to.

Hand on the doorknob, she asked "You coming?"

"Yeah." He'd probably like the idea even more if he could figure out how they'd gotten from her taking issue with everything he said to her being concerned about him riding his bike home in the storm.

THE RAIN PELTED Autumn as she raced for her car. "Still sure you don't want to leave your bike here and ride with me?" she called over her shoulder.

"I'll be fine. The house is five minutes away." A crack of thunder drowned out anything else Jon might have said.

"Suit yourself," she said to herself as she climbed into her dry car.

His bike roared to life, and he drove across the parking lot to the exit onto Hazard Cove Road. She pulled behind him. His light cotton shirt was already plastered to his broad back. A spray of water splashed up at her car as he took off fishtailing onto the road. Her breath caught. He brought the vehicle under control and headed toward the house with Autumn following at a reasonable distance.

She probably shouldn't have shot down his suggestions so quickly. They were good. There was just something about the way everyone else got in behind him that made her feel like she was losing control of the meeting, like she seemed to be losing control of her career as a midwife.

Despite her car's all-wheel drive, it hydroplaned on the slick pavement. Her heart slowed as the traction control righted the vehicle. Maybe that was her problem. Maybe she was holding on too tightly to self-control when it came to her fear of delivering babies and to other uncertainties in her life. Her fears and feeling life was veering out of control might also explain her unreasonable pettiness toward Lexi and the way her stomach had dropped when Tessa had mentioned having supper with Jon. It was a cliché, but it certainly couldn't hurt to "chill." That is, if she could.

CHAPTER 8

"**G**ood morning. Pull up a chair," Lexi said the moment Autumn entered the office. "I have the program running already so we can get right down to business."

"Hi." Autumn blinked at the bright sunlight streaming through the window where Lexi had pulled the drapes to the side. Yesterday, coming in early Saturday morning to give their assistant a crash course in medical coding had seemed like a good idea. No one would be here to interrupt. She covered her mouth to stifle a yawn. Today, after staying up late to watch a movie and tossing and turning in the heat trying to stay asleep, Autumn wasn't sure she was up to one-on-one time with their ebullient assistant.

"I'm really looking forward to the movie at Jon's house tomorrow," Lexi said. "It'll be a good way to meet some more people."

She pointed to the information Lexi needed to enter into the computer. "I have to admit that I wasn't sure about the movie idea at first, but now I'm looking forward to it, too." Since she was going to be working with Lexi all summer, she needed to get past the competitiveness that Lexi evoked in her whenever the office assistant mentioned Jon. Autumn could understand it if she had any intention of acknowledging her attraction to Jon. She didn't. She planned to keep their relationship just as it was, friends and colleagues.

The door to the office swung open, and Jon strode in. "Good. You're here."

Autumn froze, her first thought being that he was going to invite her—or Lexi—to lunch. She quickly corrected that to the more likely assumption that Jon had two mothers in labor and needed her for one of the births, which was even more unsettling.

"I need a favor."

She relaxed. *Neither*. A birth was business. For Jon business was always all business. He'd never refer to covering a birth as a favor. "What's up?"

"I need someone to pick my grandmother up at the Amtrak station. Her train gets in at about 1:15, and I have a mother who might be in late-stage labor by then. She's another one of Maureen's patients who wasn't due until after Maureen is supposed to be back from vacation."

The way Jon spoke sounded like the woman was being inconsiderate to inconvenience him by giving birth early.

"That didn't come out quite right." He motioned Autumn to the hallway off the reception area. "Excuse us," he said to Lexi. When he and Autumn were in the hall, he ran his hand over his hair. "I'm going to admit that I feel at a disadvantage delivering a woman I haven't been following throughout the pregnancy, that I don't have my own notes on."

Jon was nervous? That was a side she'd never seen before. "You were fine with Lisa," she assured him. "At the follow-up visits, both she and Greg said the birth went well."

"But you were there. You had personal knowledge of any potential complications. All I have are the medical records.

At my other practice, we met weekly to discuss our patients in case we had to cover for each other."

He was worried about complications. She'd expected him to say he felt at a disadvantage because he didn't know the mother, didn't have an established relationship with her. But that was the way she thought, not necessarily the way he did.

"Do you want me to assist at the birth?"

Indecision clouded his eyes. "No, I'd rather you meet Nana's train, if you can."

"I can." She smiled inside at what must be his childhood name for his grandmother. "I'm almost done showing Lexi the medical coding and don't have any big plans for the afternoon."

"That would be great." Relief softened his features. "I invited Nana for a visit earlier this week, and she decided to take me up on the offer immediately."

"July is prime vacation time in the Adirondacks."

"I'll give you my key so you can let her in." He pulled his keys from his lab coat pocket, removed the house key, and handed it to her. "Thanks, I appreciate this. I'll call Nana and tell her to look for you."

He took a step back toward the reception area.

"Wait. There won't be a lot of people getting off the train at Ticonderoga, but it would help if I had some idea of what your grandmother looks like."

He blinked. "Right." He reached in his other coat pocket.

She took the photo he removed from his wallet, a little surprised that he had one. Word at Samaritan had been that he was estranged from his family. The picture was of him as a young teen next to a stunning woman who looked to be in her sixties. Exceptionally good looks must run in the family.

"You can photocopy it. She still looks like that, only fifteen years older."

He didn't want her to take the photo with her. Was he

afraid she'd lose it? She handed it back. "I don't need to. I should be able to recognize her. Go on back to your mother-to-be. Your grandmother and I will be fine."

The way Lexi glanced from Jon to Autumn as they entered the waiting room from the hallway made Autumn wonder if she'd been eavesdropping.

"Thanks again," Jon said as he left.

Autumn closed the office door and turned to Lexi, who was looking up at her with her head tilted to one side. Autumn readied herself for a question or comment about Jon.

"How well do you know Josh?"

That wasn't something Autumn had not expected. "I know him and his family. I went to school with his brother. Josh was a couple of years ahead of us, so we didn't really hang out together. He served in the National Guard in Afghanistan with Dad and works for my stepmother's environmental engineering company."

Lexi laughed. "I'm still getting used to how small Paradox Lake is and how the families all know each other."

"If I think a moment, I can probably come up with more. Why do you ask?"

"When he drove me home from the meeting the other night, he invited me out to go swimming next weekend."

"Oh." Autumn silently took back all of the testy thoughts she'd had earlier about Lexi and Jon. She was never at her best when she was overtired, which wasn't a good trait in a midwife. "What did you tell him?"

"I told him I'd let him know today."

"I say go for it."

"That's what Kari and Eli said, too. I might as well have some fun while I'm here." Lexi tapped her finger on the desk. "I'm going to do it."

Autumn smiled. "Let's get the rest of your coding training

out of the way and you can give Josh a call to let him know." *And I can get to Ticonderoga to pick up Mrs. Hanlon.*

"So I enter 59400 here for global maternity care."

"That's right. It's our most-used code." Autumn showed her a few more things. "Can you finish up by yourself? Kelly will be in for a one o'clock appointment."

"Yeah, I'll be fine."

"Good because I'd better leave for the train station if I'm going to get there in time to pick up Jon's grandmother."

Autumn left a lot more confident Lexi would work out as a summer office assistant even though she didn't have any medical office experience. She was a quick learner and seemed to have gotten over her initial infatuation with Jon. Although Autumn couldn't see her and Lexi being as close as she and Kari were, they should get along fine as co-workers for the time Lexi was here.

Now, if only she was as confident about her and Jon developing a good working relationship.

Twenty minutes later, Autumn sat in a line of cars near the intersection of Route 74 and Montcalm Street watching the minutes tick toward one fifteen, the time she was supposed to pick up Jon's grandmother. She craned her neck. Traffic was halted as far as she could see, blocking the view of whatever the problem might be. No cars had passed from the other direction as long as she'd been stopped.

The car ahead of her inched back, and the driver did a U-turn so he could head back into Ticonderoga. Autumn looked at the space in front of her. She could do the same. But depending on where the problem was that could make her even later. She closed the space between her car and the car ahead and turned hers off. She should be okay calling the birthing center on her cell phone since traffic wasn't moving anyway.

"Ticonderoga Birthing center," the weekend receptionist answered.

"This is Autumn Hazard. Is Dr. Hanlon available?"

"Hi, Autumn. I'll try his office."

Autumn tapped her foot while she waited.

"Sorry, he didn't pick up. Do you want me to page him? He's probably in the birthing area. He has a mother in labor."

"No, don't page him." If he was with Maureen's mother-to-be, he wouldn't want to be interrupted by a personal call. "I'll leave a message with you and on his voice mail. If you see him within the next half hour, let him know that I'm stuck in a traffic jam, and it looks like I'll get to the train station late."

"Got it." The receptionist transferred Autumn to Jon's voicemail, and she left her message there as well.

Autumn looked up from her phone to see a county sheriff car slowing down beside her from the other way. *Great.* Using a cell phone while driving was illegal in New York. The sheriff deputy stopped and rolled down his window. Autumn did the same, breathing a sigh of relief when she recognized him from high school.

"Hi, Autumn. Are you on your way to a delivery? We're letting emergency vehicles through."

She wished she could say she was, for more reasons than the opportunity to get out of the traffic line. If she were, it would mean some normalcy in her life. "No, thanks. I'm on my way to the train station to pick up a friend's grandmother."

"Okay." He started to roll up his window.

"Wait. What happened?"

"A truck carrying chickens jackknifed. The trailer rolled over and there are chickens everywhere."

"Was anyone hurt?"

"Thankfully, no. The driver is shaken up. The EMTs are treating him."

"That's good to hear."

"We'll be getting traffic moving soon." The deputy rolled up the window and moved on.

Autumn restarted the car, and the vehicles ahead of her started moving slowly. Mrs. Hanlon would have arrived at the station about 10 minutes ago. She flexed her fingers on the steering wheel. She didn't know why she was so concerned about Jon's grandmother arriving at the station with no one to meet her. It wasn't like she was a child. And if Jon had gotten her message, he would have alerted his grandmother.

*But if he hadn't...*Autumn thought about the closeness she shared with her family, the photo Jon had showed her of him and his grandmother and the rumors she'd heard about him being estranged from his. If this visit from his grandmother was some kind of reconciliation with his family, she'd hate to do anything that might upset that.

When she finally reached her destination, Autumn rushed into the small square brick building housing the waiting area that was the Ticonderoga Amtrak station. Mrs. Hanlon sat on the polished wood bench in front of the large picture window that looked out over the parking lot. A woman about her aunt Jinx's age with two small children—the only other people at the station—glanced at her watch and out the window at the parking lot.

"Mrs. Hanlon." Autumn crossed the small room. "I'm so sorry I'm late. There was an accident and traffic was backed up."

Behind her stylish designer glasses, the older woman's eyes widened. "Excuse me. Do I know you?"

Autumn clutched her car keys in her hand. Hadn't Jon called his grandmother? "I'm Autumn Hazard. I work with

Jon. He had a birth and asked me to pick you up for him. Didn't he call?" Her words tumbled out without a breath between them.

"Oh, no. I turned my phone off." Jon's grandmother reached into the Burberry bag on the bench beside her and took out her phone. "Yes, he called and texted me your picture."

Jon had a picture of her on his phone? When could he have taken that, and why?

"A link to your picture," Mrs. Hanlon corrected herself. "On the birthing center website. You're a midwife."

"Yes." She still was, technically, even if she hadn't delivered any babies on her own for several months. "I did my clinicals at Samaritan Hospital when Jon was a resident there."

A warm smile reminiscent of Jon's lady-killer one spread across her face. "So, you're old friends."

Autumn wasn't sure that's the way she'd describe their relationship. Their friendship was still developing. "Do you have luggage?"

Mrs. Hanlon pointed at a large family-sized suitcase Autumn had assumed belonged to the other woman. Either Mrs. Hanlon had a tendency to really over pack or was planning on a long visit.

"Will you and the kids be okay here by yourself?" Mrs. Hanlon addressed the other traveler. We can wait until your husband gets here." She looked at Autumn for a confirmation.

"Of course." The station was a little isolated, outside of Ticonderoga proper, on the edge of the Fort Ticonderoga historic site property. "If your husband is coming Route 74, he probably got stuck in the same traffic I did."

"Thanks, but you don't have to stay. I see him pulling in now." She pointed to the parking lot.

"It was nice meeting you," Mrs. Hanlon said. "And I wish you the best with your house hunting." She turned to Autumn. "Her husband recently took a job in Ticonderoga, and she and the kids are here for a week to look at houses."

"I think you'll like it here. The area's a great place to raise kids," Autumn said. "Of course, I'm biased. I grew up on Paradox Lake about 20 minutes from here."

"Thanks. The mountains are pretty, but it's a lot more isolated than where we live now."

"It's all what you're used to." Autumn remembered counting the time until her clinicals would be finished and she could move back up north where she could live a more isolated lifestyle.

Autumn reached for Mrs. Hanlon's suitcase handle.

"You don't have to do that," the older woman said.

"Yes, I do." She shot her a quick smile.

Jon's grandmother went ahead and opened the door for her. As Autumn wrestled the suitcase out to the car, she eyed the diminutive elderly woman with admiration, thankful that the luggage had wheels. The woman must work out daily to have handled the case herself on the trip up here.

While Mrs. Hanlon made herself comfortable in the passenger seat, Autumn stashed the suitcase in the back seat. No way would it fit in the trunk with her equipment and the twins' swim toys, which she'd never taken out. Her cell phone rang as she opened the driver's door. She frowned at the display. *The birthing center*. Was Jon calling to check up on her and his grandmother? Hadn't he gotten her message?

"Hello."

"Autumn, it's Lexi. Kelly called a couple of minutes ago to see if you were still here. She and Kari are at Tanya's. Tanya's little boy was born this morning. Anyway, Allie and her husband are on their way here, and Kelly wants you to come and be with them until she can get to the center. She'll be here as soon as she can."

"I'm at the train station. There was an accident and I had to wait in traffic. I still need to drop Mrs. Hanlon off at Jon's house. It'll be forty or forty-five minutes before I get back to Ticonderoga. "Allie should be fine until I arrive. And Jon's there."

"Okay, I'll let Kelly and admissions know."

"And call Kristen in if she's not there already. She can be with Allie until I get there."

"She's right here. See you in a bit." Lexi clicked off.

"Is there a problem?" Mrs. Hanlon asked.

Autumn explained what was going on.

"I can wait at the birthing center. It's not like I haven't spent many hours touring medical facilities with my husband or waiting on him while he conducted JMH business."

Autumn wasn't sure where the bitterness in Mrs. Hanlon's voice was coming from, but it would make things easier for her if she could go directly to the birthing center. "That would be good if you really don't mind. Jon has a mother in labor, so I can't tell you when he'll be available. But I'm just going to stay with one of our mothers until the other midwife arrives. Then I can take you to the house."

"I make sure I always have a book to read." Mrs. Hanlon tapped the eReader protruding from the pocket in the side of her leather purse. The resigned look on her face almost made Autumn change her mind and drive out to Paradox Lake first.

They arrived at the birthing center 10 minutes later. Autumn's parents-to-be were checking in with the receptionist. After greeting them, Autumn introduced Mrs. Hanlon to the receptionist and asked her to make the older woman comfortable in the staff lounge. She sensed Mrs.

Hanlon watching her and was glad when she and the parents turned the corner to the birthing suite.

JON WALKED through the lobby and frowned when he saw no one in the reception area. He was going to have to talk with the office manager. But not right now. He was in too good of a mood. The delivery had gone well, almost as perfectly as the one with Autumn the other day. All that had been missing was the atmosphere of closeness Autumn and that couple had shared. Plus, his grandmother was here for a visit, and he'd had a call earlier in the day from the director of Help for Haiti saying they had received his C.V. and were very interested in his joining the nonprofit organization when his one-year contract with the Ticonderoga Birthing Center was over.

"Nana." He started when he entered his office and found his grandmother sitting in his desk chair reading. "What are you doing here? I thought Autumn was driving you to my house." Jon's bored his gaze into hers. "Did *Grandfather* ask you to check out the facility?"

"No, but I'm sure he would have if I'd given him enough notice of my visit for him to think of it." She closed her eReader and placed it on the desk. "As for why I'm waiting in your office, your friend got a call to come here and cover for another midwife until she returned from a home birth. I found that interesting, that they do home births."

"I'm sorry. I know how you feel about hanging around medical facilities." Jon was well aware of his grandfather's propensity of turning any trip he and Nana took into a business trip. "Autumn should have had you wait in the lounge. It's more comfortable."

"She did, but I wanted to check out your office. For

myself," she added. "I asked the receptionist to tell Autumn I'm in here when she comes to get me. She seems very nice."

Yes, nice was one adjective he'd use to describe Autumn. Beautiful was another, but he wasn't about to share that with Nana.

"She said she's known you since you were a resident." His grandmother's eyes twinkled. "Do I see a cause and effect?"

"What?"

"Did you take the position here because of Autumn?"

"No."

"You don't have to bark at me. You sounded like your grandfather."

"Sorry." The last thing he wanted was to be in any way like his grandfather.

"I only asked because it's an administrative position. You've always said how much you like delivering babies."

"I should get to do plenty of births here if the past few days have been any indication. As the center's administrator, I seem to be the back-up obstetrician for every doctor and midwife in a 50-mile radius." He wasn't going to share that the reason he took the job was for the administrative experience. He'd need it working with Help for Haiti. He and Nana didn't disagree on many important issues. But his following in his cousin Angie's footsteps and pursuing work in Haiti was one that they did.

His office door opened, interrupting the conversation.

"Mrs. Hanlon, I apologize. It took Kelly longer to get here than she'd expected." Autumn halted. "Jon."

He fought the grin that her wide-eyed surprise brought to his lips.

"How did your birth go?" She regained her composure.

"Textbook perfect."

"See. You were concerned about nothing."

His face warmed. He glanced sidewise at his grandmother to see her reaction to Autumn's words. Hanlon men never admitted doubts about their abilities in anything, particularly work. Nana had a familiar all-knowing expression on her face.

"As I said this morning, I would have liked more background on the case." He didn't know why he was explaining himself.

"I know what you mean. I felt like that for my first couple of births after I joined Kelly's practice. I hadn't been with the mothers for most of their pregnancies."

Jon reached for Nana's suitcase. For some reason, Autumn's words rankled him. He brushed them off. Nana wasn't his father or grandfather. She wouldn't care if he'd expressed concerns to Autumn, or anyone else. What was with him? All Autumn was doing was commiserating with him, like any colleague might.

"I'm free for the rest of the day if you still want me to drive your grandmother to your place." Autumn exchanged a glance with Nana.

"No, thanks. I'm cleared for the afternoon now, too."

"Okay. It was nice meeting you, Mrs. Hanlon. I'm sure I'll see you again before you go. I live on the other side of the duplex Jon is renting."

"Oh, I'm sure you will."

The way Nana's voice rose at the end of her statement told Jon she hadn't taken his "no" to her question about whether Autumn had been a factor in his coming to the Ticonderoga center at face value.

Jon watched the door close behind Autumn. He'd have to clear things up with Nana, convince her that Autumn was nothing more than a colleague. He lifted the suitcase. Its weight matched its size. "Ready?"

His grandmother stood and nodded toward the case. "It has wheels."

"I've got it." He rethought his immediate reaction to carry the suitcase anyway and lowered it to the floor. There was no need to impress Nana.

"I'm having the rest of my things shipped," she said, as they left his office and walked down the hall to the parking lot door. "The train didn't have checked luggage."

She had more things? Nana was a no-nonsense person. It was out of character for her to bring more than she'd absolutely need for her visit. She seemed her usual self, but he made a mental note to keep an eye out for any other personality changes. Although she was in good physical health, Nana would be turning 80 on her next birthday.

"How long are you planning to stay?" he asked, stopping to hold the door open for her.

"Indefinitely. I've left your grandfather."

CHAPTER 9

*J*on filched one of the chocolate chip cookies Nana had baked for the trivia group movie this afternoon and left the plate covered on the kitchen counter. In the two weeks since she'd arrived, he'd gotten no further in knowing why she'd entrenched herself at his house or when she might be planning to leave. She changed the subject whenever he brought it or his grandfather up. The fact that she'd bought herself a car this week at the dealer in Ticonderoga said her departure probably wasn't imminent. The only word he'd gotten from the rest of his family were two terse voicemail messages, one from his father and one from his grandfather, telling him to make Nana go home. As if that was something he could readily do.

He leaned against the counter and finished his cookie, enjoying being alone for a while. Nana had gone to church and the grocery store afterwards. It wasn't that he minded sharing the house with Nana, per se, but he was used to living alone and doing things his way. He knew she didn't do it on purpose, but at times, she made him feel twelve years old.

The wall phone rang, and he pushed away from the counter to reach over and answer it. "Hello."

"Jon, this is Becca. I hate to do this at the last minute, but I'm going to have to cancel on the meeting. My daughter has been sick to her stomach since early this morning."

"What are her symptoms? Does she have diarrhea? There have been a couple of cases of *E.coli* at the Saranac Lake medical center."

"More likely a sugar-overload tummy ache. Before I got up, she got into a bag of candy I thought I had put away out of her reach and without her knowledge."

"If she's not feeling better tomorrow, you may want to take her to your doctor. You can't be too careful."

"I'm sure she'll be fine. I feel badly that I have to cancel after you had that birth last Sunday, and we had to put off the movie until today. I know Autumn's put a lot of effort into getting the group up and going."

"Mommy! Ari threw up on the chair." Becca's son's voice came over the phone.

"I have to go. Bye."

He hoped Becca was right about it being nothing more than too much candy. *E.coli* was more likely to cause diarrhea than vomiting. But even simple illnesses could lead to serious complications. His throat tightened, as had happened with Angie. He shook off the weight settling on his shoulders. Angie had been on his mind too much the past few days, ever since he'd received the literature from Help for Haiti in the mail.

A knock on the front door drew him into the living room. Autumn stood on the other side of the screen door smiling. The last of his gloom lifted.

"Come in. It's open." He started across the room.

She held up a large plastic bottle of iced tea she'd said

she'd bring to go with the cookies and a Zester grater to show him her hands were full.

He pushed the door open. She had on a flowing skirt and red t-shirt. He admired how the skirt emphasized the graceful way she moved when she walked in.

"Hi. Your grandmother asked if I had a Zester she could borrow. Is she in the kitchen?"

"No, she's at the grocery store." He took the tea and grater from her and placed the tea on the coffee table next to the stack of red plastic cups and napkins he'd put out before Becca had called.

"Your grandmother certainly is getting involved for a summer visitor."

He thought so, too. "Did she tell you that, that she's here for the summer?"

Autumn bit her lip. "Not in so many words."

"She's enjoying herself, and my grandfather is on a business trip." Grandfather was always on a business trip or planning one, so his statement couldn't be too far off. "So she's extended her visit." For how long was anyone's guess. She evaded his question every time he asked. "Make yourself comfortable. I'll put the grater in the kitchen and get the cookies Nana made for us."

He grabbed the plate of cookies and left the grater in its place on the counter. As Autumn had noticed, Nana was settling in at Paradox Lake nicely. *Too nicely.* Because he knew how difficult his grandfather could be, he could see how his grandmother might want some time away from him. But Nana couldn't hide out in the mountains indefinitely. At some point, Grandfather would storm up here to take her back. That could be Nana's plan, to see if Grandfather cared enough to come after her.

"Hey, you're not eating all those cookies are you?" Autumn called from the other room. Her voice grew louder.

"They smelled delicious when your grandmother was baking them yesterday. I hoped they were for us." She met him at the doorway.

"They taste as good as they smell," he said. "I sampled them earlier. I couldn't serve my friends inferior cookies."

"Of course not. I'd better double check."

He lifted the plastic wrap to offer her a cookie and his hand brushed hers as she reached for one. Her eyes darkened, locking his gaze to hers. She snatched the cookie and popped a bite in her mouth. He watched her slowly chew it, obviously savoring the sweet flavor while he enjoyed the delight she took in each chew.

"Jay, I'm home." The screen door clicked closed behind his grandmother. She looked from Autumn to him. "I didn't mean to interrupt."

"You're not interrupting anything."

"I was just sampling one of your delicious cookies." Autumn took a step back from the cookie plate and him.

"Good. Jay, I mean Jon—I keep forgetting he prefers Jon. We always called him Jay to distinguish him from his grandfather. Jon and I are still working out our living arrangements. I don't want to intrude on his privacy."

Autumn wrinkled her brow.

He understood her confusion. Nana was talking as if she planned to stay with him permanently and he and Autumn had something to be private about. As much as he loved his grandmother and wished he could have lived with her when he was a child, he'd never imagined he'd get his childhood wish now.

"Have you changed your plans?" Nana asked.

"No, I don't know what you mean."

"You said your trivia group was coming over to watch a movie." Nana made a point of glancing around the living room, stopping with him and Autumn standing in the doorway.

"We are," Autumn answered for him. "I'm the first one here."

And maybe the only one coming, considering it was 10 minutes past the time they'd agreed to meet. Not that he'd mind being alone with Autumn. He snapped his thoughts back to the conversation. "Becca called. She can't come. Her little girl is sick."

"That's too bad," Autumn said. "I hope it's nothing serious."

"She said it was probably too much candy. But I told her about the two cases of *E.coli* at the medical center."

"You didn't."

His jaw tightened. "I thought she should know. The county health department hasn't determined the cause."

"Why did she need to know? The two people who were admitted to the medical center were campers from a campground on Saranac Lake. Becca's daughter hasn't been anywhere near there. I hope you didn't cause her unnecessary worry."

His grandmother placed her hand on his forearm, as she'd often done when he and his father were talking, and she'd feared it would turn into an argument. It was her signal to back off a lost cause. He resisted shaking it off. He was old enough to pick his own battles. Of course, it didn't make any sense to him, either, to be arguing with Autumn. What she'd said was true, and he generally reserved confrontations for family members.

"Becca," Nana said. "She's a petite dark-haired woman with two kids, an older boy and a toddler girl?"

"Yes, Becca Norton," Autumn answered.

"Norton." Nana put a finger to her lip. "I met her mother, or maybe it was mother-in-law, at the meeting today."

"That would be her ex-mother-in-law," Autumn said.

Jon eyed the TV across the room and listened for any sound of other people arriving. This was the point where Nana normally would say something about how too many people his and Autumn's age didn't make enough of an effort to keep their marriages together.

Nana simply nodded. At least she wasn't going to be a hypocrite, assuming she'd really left his grandfather. Heaven knew Nana had put her all into her marriage.

"I'm getting to know everyone. Give me another few weeks and I should have it all down. Everyone I've met has been so friendly and welcoming, nothing like what you hear about small towns being insular and closed to people from outside."

"We have our share of narrow-minded people, just like anywhere else. I think the dependence on tourists may make us more open," Autumn said.

"I like it here. How about you, Jon?"

"I don't know." His ears had shut down at *another few weeks*.

Autumn's eyes narrowed.

What had he said?

"You're probably so busy working that you haven't taken time to get to know all these nice people. I'm afraid his father and grandfather have set a bad example for him in that regard," his grandmother explained to Autumn. "His mother, too, for that matter."

He caught on to the gist of the conversation. "I joined the trivia group."

"Which seems to consist of you and Autumn, who you already know."

He hadn't come to Paradox Lake and the birthing center to make new friends. Nana's dig about not socializing more took him back to his awkward middle school days when he'd preferred reading science journals and science fiction to spending time with his classmates. His parents were fine with his behavior. It kept him quiet and out of their ways. Nana hadn't been. She'd joined the parents' organization at his private school and made him go to any and all social functions. By high school, he'd outgrown his awkwardness and discovered girls and they'd discovered him. He still generally preferred his books, though. They didn't ask him for companionship and commitment he didn't know how to give.

AUTUMN GLANCED AT THE DOOR. "Josh said he and Lexi were coming when I talked with him the other day."

"Maybe they changed their plans," Mrs. Hanlon picked up her eReader from the table. "I'm going out to the patio to read and leave you two alone to watch your movie," Mrs. Hanlon said.

Jon threw yet another frown his grandmother's way. While Autumn could sympathize with his irritation at his grandmother's remark about leaving them alone, she couldn't figure out what else was with him. He'd invited his grandmother for a visit, and he'd seemed happy that she was coming when he'd asked Autumn to pick Mrs. Hanlon up at the train station. Now he didn't want her here?

"I apologize for Nana. And maybe the movie idea wasn't as good as it sounded to everyone at the meeting the other week."

Now she knew something was up with Jon. The know-it-all-resident she'd worked with at Samaritan would have phrased his idea being a bust in a way that would have put him in a better light. "No need to apologize. My grand-mother is the same way about any male friends I introduce her to. As for getting a group together, July isn't the greatest time to do that, with vacations and all." She needn't admit that she hadn't done much better launching the group in the spring. She held a bit of resentment that Jon had commandeered her group with his movie suggestion.

"Hello, hate to interrupt, but someone told us the trivia group was meeting here today," Lexi said.

Autumn didn't miss Lexi's emphasis on the word interrupt and, from the brief hardening of Jon's features, the veiled reference to her and Jon being alone hadn't been lost on him either. Why did everyone think she and Jon had something going on? Despite their birthing suite kiss, nothing more than friendship was going to develop between them. They were too different. She was the settling down type and he wasn't.

"That's what I heard, too. Come on in. Autumn and I were putting out the refreshments and wondering where you two were."

"We didn't mean to be late," Josh said.

Jon wiggled his eyebrows in response, making them all laugh. She was entirely too sensitive about people thinking she and Jon were a couple, about everything lately.

Lexi smiled up at her apparent date. "Josh took me to lunch at his mother's and we all got talking and lost track of time. His grandmother was there. She's a hoot."

"She sure is," Autumn said. "I had Mrs. Stowe for English in high school, as did my aunt and my dad, and maybe my grandparents, too."

"Get out," Josh said. "Grandma's not that old."

"She'd only have to be four or five years older than my grandparents to have been their English teacher," Autumn retorted. "I'm going to have to ask them."

"You do that. But I think I'm right."

"We'll see about that."

"We should start the movie." Jon's statement sounded almost like a reprimand.

What was that about? She and Josh were only teasing each other, not arguing or purposely delaying the movie. Jon was altogether too serious too much of the time, at least when she was around him. It made her wonder about the stories she'd heard at Samaritan about his dating escapades. He didn't strike her as a particularly fun date. Could have been his money they found so fun. While Jon put the DVD in the player, she examined her thoughts. She was probably reacting to the small turnout today and the feeling she was being pushed at him. He'd only wanted to start the movie.

Lexi and Josh sat on the couch, leaving a well-used recliner and a less comfortable looking side chair. Autumn took the side chair, figuring the recliner was Jon's usual TV watching spot.

Jon pressed the play button on the remote.

"Should we wait for your grandmother? We saw her outside when we drove up," Lexi said.

"No." Jon skipped the advertising at the start of the DVD.

Autumn rubbed her skirt fabric between her thumb and forefinger. "She's already seen the series, so she went out to the patio to read."

"Wasn't Becca going to come? I know Tessa couldn't get anyone to cover the theater matinee today."

Lexi was certainly full of questions. From the cozy look of her and Josh on the couch, she might be trying to draw the afternoon with Josh out as long as possible, and Autumn couldn't blame her. Josh was a really nice guy.

"She called Jon and said she couldn't come because her daughter was sick."

"That's too bad," Lexi said.

Jon paused the movie. "Are we ready to watch?"

The next two hours passed quickly.

"That was good." Josh looked down at Lexi, his eyes soft.

"If you have a minute, I have something else to talk about." Jon pushed the recliner upright and picked up some brochures on the table next to him. He leaned forward. "I was thinking that while I'm here at the birthing center, I'd like to do something more to promote women's health. A community effort, and you're my community so far. This is some information about Help for Haiti that I got in the mail." He passed a brochure to the others. "I was looking at the 'Sponsor a Medical Professional' campaign."

Josh tapped his leg with the brochure. "That's a pretty lofty goal for the few of us in the trivia group to undertake."

"We could make it long term." Jon spoke as if the campaign was a done deal. "And bring some community groups in."

"Yeah." Autumn got caught up in his enthusiasm as she skimmed the brochure Josh had handed her. "Make it a competition. In my limited experience, fund raising competitions always do well."

"No, not a competition," Jon shot back. Different community groups wouldn't be balanced in terms of numbers.".

"Not by group. Women versus men." Autumn looked from face to face.

"I like it." Lexi poked Josh with her elbow.

"You think you women can beat us men?" Josh asked. "Count me in. Great idea, Jon."

"The competition was Autumn's idea, not mine," Jon said.

Autumn frowned. All the enthusiasm had drained from Jon. Something about having a competition wasn't sitting well with him.

"Help for Haiti is only a suggestion. You guys might have a better idea." He walked over to the DVD player, ejected the movie, and put it in the case.

"Not me," Lexi said.

"Nor me," John agreed.

"I like it, too." Autumn scanned the brochure a second time. "Why don't I call Becca and Tessa later and make it unanimous."

"I don't like the idea of making it a competition," Jon said. "But I'll go with whatever the rest of you decide."

"Then it's a go, as long as Becca and Tessa agree." Lexi rubbed her hands together and looked sidewise at Josh. "I can't wait for the kickoff."

"I can scout out some other groups." Autumn looked for the spark she'd seen in Jon's eyes when he'd passed out the brochures to return, and her heart sank when it didn't. Jon couldn't be that put out about a little friendly competition. "Do you want to help me, since you're familiar with the local organizations?"

"Sure, I'll help," he said.

A lukewarm response if there was one. She'd made the competition suggestion to support Jon, not shoot him down.

"Hey, how was your movie?" Mrs. Hanlon breezed into the room from outside.

While Lexi and Josh answered her, Jon leaned down, scooped up the remaining brochures and stuffed them in the back pocket of his jeans, pulling his t-shirt down over them.

He didn't want his grandmother to see the brochures? That was strange and futile. The rest of them had copies in their hands. Whatever was between him and his grandmother was none of Autumn's business. With her employment contract up soon and her still not feeling confident about birthing babies, she had enough problems of her own. She didn't need to take on anyone else's. Autumn dropped her hand holding the brochure between her leg and the chair's armrest where Mrs. Hanlon wouldn't see it.

"Thanks for the cookies and tea," Lexi said. She and Josh stood to leave.

Autumn rose, too.

"Can you stay a minute?" Jon asked.

Lexi shot her a grin.

Autumn knew Lexi was well-meaning, but she irritated her anyway. Jon probably wanted to go over how they'd present the project to other groups or, maybe, share why he was so resistant to the idea of a male-female fundraising competition.

Once the other couple was outside and out of ear shot, Jon picked up a postcard from the table where the flyers had been earlier. "I wanted to wait until after the movie. Did you get one of these?" He handed her the card.

Autumn didn't have to look at it. She'd received a similar one from her former roommate. A save-the-date announcement for Kate's October wedding in St. Croix. "Yes."

Jon snorted. "I can tell by your expression you can't figure out why I got one, either."

"You two didn't part on good terms." She handed the card back.

He slapped it against the side of his leg. "You've only heard Kate's version of our breakup. Sit. Please." He motioned her to the couch and joined her there.

Autumn twisted the Haiti flyer in her lap. "Kate told me she loved you and thought you loved her. She was making plans."

"I never told her I loved her. That's not something I'd toss out lightly."

That wasn't the impression Autumn had gotten at Samaritan, but knowing Jon better now, she believed him.

"And I heard about the plans Kate was making through the Samaritan gossip mill, not from her. That's why I broke things off with her. Because she hadn't been straight with me. When we started dating, she said she wasn't looking for anything serious."

"She could have changed her mind as she got to know you better." Autumn knew she had. "Fell in love with you."

"No, believe me, the only thing Kate was in love with was my family name and money."

"Then why didn't you stop all of the nasty things people said about you?" She had to ask, although knowing Kate, what he'd said had a ring of truth to it. Kate was into drama in real life.

"People will say what they want to say, and I knew my friends, the people who counted, wouldn't believe her lies."

Autumn untwisted the flyer and smoothed it on her lap. When Jon hadn't corrected the gossip, she'd believed it, at least in part.

"You don't have to say anything. When I got the postcard, I thought that if we're going to be working together at the center and spending time together in the trivia group, I should give you my side, put us at a fresh start." Jon leaned forward with a look of yearning in his eyes. "I like you. I'd like to be friends."

A wave of regret washed over her. She should have known better than to take the Samaritan gossip at face value and to leap to the conclusion he was living up to his Samaritan player reputation dating Becca and Tessa here. She hadn't seen or heard anything to actually support that conclusion. "Thanks for sharing."

His eyes brightened, confirming her perception that she didn't have to say she believed him. "And we're already friends."

He grinned and flicked his forefinger against the postcard. "Friend to friend, my take on the postcard is that Kate sent it to say she'd done as well—better—without me."

Autumn nodded in agreement. "I know it's not nice, but I

thought Kate sent the card to brag, too. She has to know there's no way I could swing attending her wedding in St. Croix."

Jon placed his hand over hers, sending a jolt of awareness —of his maleness, his nearness, his sincerity—through her. "Don't feel badly. Kate is Kate."

He was right. She slipped her hand out from under his. "I should get going."

"Right." He stared at his hand on her leg for a moment before jerking it back.

She rose and Jon followed her to the door. "See you at work."

Autumn hurried across the slate walkway to her side of the house. As if her expiring work contract and fear of delivering babies weren't enough, she had another problem now. She was running out of reasons to distance herself from Jon.

CHAPTER 10

"*A*ll right. Why are you two double teaming me?" Kari asked when she arrived for the meeting Autumn had called. "If it's about last week, Kristen was more than happy to take that birth for me so I could fill in for the camp nurse at Sunrise. I'm not complaining, but I miss having summers free to be with the kids at the camp."

"That was fine," Kelly assured her.

Kari paled. "If it's not about work, it's the baby, and it can't be good, not with both of you here."

"Don't jump to conclusions," Kelly said.

Autumn lifted her gaze to the ceiling. This was Kari's fourth pregnancy, and she was their primary delivery nurse. Kelly should have realized Kari would be suspicious about this meeting, made on short notice, with Kelly joining them.

"You know your blood sugar has been running high," Autumn started.

"It's been more normal this week. I've been checking it myself." Kari's eyes widened. "You're not going to put me on insulin, are you? With the other three, I controlled it with diet. I'll be more careful, assign Eli as my food guard. He's well-trained at giving orders.

Autumn raised her hand palm out to stop her. "I'm concerned. I don't know why diet isn't working this time." She hesitated. "I'm going to order more tests, but to me it looks like insulin might be necessary."

Autumn caught Kelly's frown. What did she expect? At Kari's insistence, Autumn was still Kari's midwife. And Kari understood what was going on. She wouldn't have asked about insulin if she hadn't thought that was where the conversation was headed. Why wouldn't she be straightforward with Kari, who was a friend and knew nearly as much about pregnancy and birth as Autumn and Kelly? She'd be straightforward with any of her mothers.

"I see." Kari was quiet for a moment. "You know I wouldn't do anything to jeopardize this baby." She touched her rounded belly.

"I know, and neither would I...we." Autumn had to include Kelly, even though Kelly had indicated she'd wait a while longer before referring Kari out of the practice.

"Autumn asked me to talk with Jon about transferring you to his care for the rest of your pregnancy," Kelly said.

That wasn't exactly right. She'd convinced Kelly that Kari's pregnancy needed to be supervised by a doctor. Kelly had taken it on herself to talk with Jon before Autumn had had a chance to.

"I have an appointment," Kelly said. "I'll leave you to make the arrangements with Jon's office.

The door closed behind Kelly. "I have to switch, don't I? I can't convince you that I'll be more careful?" Kari sighed. "What if the new tests don't show that I need insulin?"

"I think you need to be followed by a doctor. It doesn't have to be Jon. Is there someone at the medical center in Saranac that you'd rather use?"

"If it's my choice, I'd rather continue to see you. I figured by the time this one is ready to pop, I'd have you convinced to do the delivery."

Her heart heavy, Autumn shook her head. She wished she had the confidence in herself that Kari had in her.

"Be straight with me," Kari said.

"I always am."

"Is this about Suzy Hill? Are you being overly cautious because of what happened?"

"Kelly thinks I am being overly cautious. She advised me to wait another month and see. I disagree. And if I'd caught any problems with Suzy's pregnancy earlier, she and Jack would be busy planning that houseful of kids they wanted." Her throat clogged. "Rather than telling everyone they're happy with having only one child."

"They're already at work on that."

"What do you mean? Suzy can't have any more children."

"Jack's mother told me at church last week that he and Suzy have applied to become foster parents."

"They'd be very good. But you're avoiding the main topic here. Your and your baby's health."

"Yes, I'll see Jon, only I want to see you, too. Can you do that?"

"I have no objections. It's not my decision, though. It's Jon's. I'll talk with him." Kari was a good friend. She wished she could assure her that it would be no problem. She and Jon had worked well together when Lisa and Greg's baby was born. But Lisa was one of her and Kelly's mothers. Jon had been covering for Kelly. It could be a different story if Kari became Jon's patient. He might see Autumn as interfering with his practice.

"Do you want Eli and me to talk with Jon before we leave on vacation this weekend? Tell him what we want? Eli will back me."

"I know he will." The retired Air Force Captain would go to the ends of the Earth for Kari and her kids. He'd be a good match up against Jon. What was she thinking? Jon wasn't the enemy. "I'll take care of it." And she hoped she could.

JON SAW the message light on his desk phone flashing as he said good-bye to his last patient of the day, a nervous first-time mother who, in his opinion, had too many family members giving her pregnancy advice.

He picked up the phone and played the message. "Jon, Autumn. Do you have time today to talk about Kari? Let me know. I'm in the office now and will be home after two." Autumn followed with her home phone number, which he jotted on his desk pad, even though he had it in his cell phone contacts.

He disconnected the call and punched in Autumn's number, tapping his pen on the desk to count the rings… five, six, seven, eight. He finally got a breathless "hello."

"Autumn, Jon."

"Hi, let me catch my breath. I was out back when I heard the phone."

"You wanted to talk about Kari?"

"Yes, what's your schedule look like for tomorrow?"

"Jammed. I have an induction scheduled, unless the mother goes into labor tonight on her own, and a home visit, along with a couple of appointments."

"A home visit, eh?"

The smile in her voice warmed him. "Yes, I've given my patients that option and most of them have been receptive to adding that to their birth plans."

"What about the day after tomorrow?"

"That would be okay, but if you want, I'm free now. I

could stop by when I get home." As he said the words, he remembered his grandmother's insinuation that he was a workaholic. "Unless you'd rather meet day after tomorrow at the birthing center."

"No, here is fine. I can access Kari's records on my iPad."

"Fine." He hesitated. "Do you have dinner plans?"

"Nooo." She drew out the word.

"Then I'll pick up a couple of subs at the Paradox General Store on my way home." When she didn't respond right away, he added "It's a business expense."

"I'd double check with your accountant about that," she teased.

"What kind do you want?"

"I really like their veggie sub."

"I should have known. The veggie pizza."

The phone went quiet.

"At the camp, with your family." How or why had he remembered that?

"Oh, yeah."

He brushed away the prick of disappointment. So what if she wasn't impressed that he'd remembered. They were talking about a business appointment not a date. "I'll be there in about a half hour."

AUTUMN HUNG up the phone and touched her hair. She'd tied it on top of her head to get it out the way and could feel countless strands straying from the knot. She splayed her fingers in front of her. They were covered with green weed stains. Her gaze dropped to the dirt on her knees. She must look a mess. Not at all professional. That's what this meeting was, she reminded herself, a professional meeting, even though it was at her house and Jon was bringing dinner.

She raced around the living room, picking up her break-fast coffee cup from the end table and stashing the novel she was reading in the bookcase. She eyed the faux Oriental area rug and the clock. There might be time to give it a quick sweep before Jon arrived. Or not. He was a guy. He wouldn't notice whether her rug was vacuumed. But she did need to change out of her grimy shorts and t-shirt and clean herself up.

A knock sounded at the door as she finished touching up her makeup. Jon was here sooner than she'd expected him. She glanced in the mirror at the sleeveless cotton top and tan linen slacks she'd chosen. The right touch of business and casual.

She came down the stairs and saw Mrs. Hanlon at the door. "Hi." She let the older woman in.

"I'll only stay a minute. I know Jon is on his way. He called. Since I'd already baked these blackberry tarts for us, I thought I'd bring a couple of them over for your dinner. You haven't already made a dessert, have you?"

"No."

"Good." Mrs. Hanlon handed Autumn two tarts. She tilted her head and sniffed. "What are you making, not that it matters. Jon isn't picky about food."

"Jon is picking up subs. This is a business meeting. I need to discuss a mother that we're transitioning to his care."

"Oh." The older woman's disappointment was clear.

She must have thought I'd invited Jon for dinner.

"I think you're good for Jon, whether as a friend, a colleague or more. Your family, too. The exposure to healthier family dynamics than our dysfunctional one. I was once a social worker. You'd think I could have done a better job with my family."

Autumn cleared her throat. She didn't really need to hear the Hanlon family history right now, but she didn't want to be rude to Mrs. Hanlon. She liked her. "The tarts look…" She bent her head. "And smell delicious."

Mrs. Hanlon waved her off. "Baking is something I do when I'm thinking, frustrated or angry. Over the years, I've gotten very good at it. Today, I was thinking."

"Too bad you won't be around for the Paradox Lake Fall Festival. Mrs. Stowe would certainly appreciate your contributions to the bake sale."

"Well, I may be around. Tell me, is the woman you're referring to Jon having a lot of difficulties? Is there a danger he could lose her or the baby?"

"Mrs. Hanlon, you know I can't answer that."

"It was worth trying. I'm going to tell you something about Jon. He likes the challenges of high-risk pregnancies, or thinks he does. What he really needs is some happy normal births so he can see the real joy of new life. Birth isn't an enemy that has to be conquered."

Autumn didn't know how to respond. From what she'd seen, she couldn't disagree. Jon did like the challenge of high-risk pregnancies and births and took joy in making the births successful. There had to be something behind Mrs. Hanlon's words. Whatever that something was, she'd leave it to Jon to share if he chose to. Maybe once they'd worked together longer.

"I like that you took Jon with you on a home visit. That opened his eyes some."

"I don't know about that, but he did say that he has a home follow-up with one of his mothers tomorrow."

"Yes!" Mrs. Hanlon fist pumped, a reaction Autumn would more expect from her eight-year-old brother than a woman of Mrs. Hanlon's age and position.

The rumble of Jon's bike approaching the house caused both of the women to look out the door.

"I'll slip out the back," Mrs. Hanlon said. "Enjoy your

dinner. If you're looking for something to do after your meeting, that Sherlock Holmes program Jon likes is on tonight."

She liked the program, too. Maybe...*No.* As she'd told his grandmother, Jon was coming over to talk business. She'd wait for him to make the first move if he wanted more.

"Thanks. I'll bring the tart pans back tomorrow," Autumn said.

"Any time." Mrs. Hanlon disappeared into the kitchen.

"The door's open," Autumn said when Jon jogged up the steps.

He walked in and his gaze went directly to the tarts that filled Autumn's hands. "Nana?"

"Yes, she thought they'd go perfectly with our dinner, whatever I was making."

"I should have been clearer when I called. You'll like the tarts. They're my favorite dessert."

"Mine's chocolate-vanilla swirl soft-serve ice cream. My family celebrates everything with a trip to the soft-serve stand." One of those healthier family dynamics Mrs. Hanlon wanted Jon exposed to? "I'm sure I'll love the tarts, as much as I did the cookies. If your grandmother stays much longer, I'll have to buy an all-new wardrobe in a larger size."

Jon looked her over, sending a ripple of pleasure through her. "Or I could roust you out at six in the morning to run with me."

"Six a.m.? No thanks. I'll come up with some other way to work off the calories."

"Don't say I didn't offer to help. I thought we could eat first. I ordered a hot sub. Then we can discuss the case."

Autumn cringed hearing Kari referred to as a case. But she wasn't going to let semantics get their collaboration off on the wrong foot. "Kitchen or patio for eating?"

"Kitchen. I wouldn't put it past Nana to be 'supervising'

us on the patio from the yard while she worked on the flower beds."

"She does watch out for you. Are you her only grand-child? I was for a long time, and it is quite a responsibility."

Rather than the laugh Autumn expected, Jon's expression went dead serious. "No, there are—were—five of us. My cousin Angie died almost seven years ago. And one great grandchild. Angie had a little boy."

"How sad. How old is he?"

"He's six. When I was downstate, I tried to see him as often as I could and take him to Nana's house. Angie and I spent a lot of time there when we were growing up."

"Me, too, about spending a lot of time at my grandpar-ents'. Dad and I lived with them until I went to college."

"I thought you went to the community college."

Jon remembered what kind of pizza she liked and where she'd gone to college? She shifted the weight of the tarts. "A friend and I had an apartment in Ticonderoga."

His stomach growled. "Enough talk. Time to eat."

They went into the kitchen and had their subs. Autumn crumpled her wrapper when she'd finished. "I'm stuffed. Would you mind having the tarts after we talk? I could make coffee or tea."

"Fine with me."

"My iPad is in the living room."

Jon pulled out his notebook and sat in the center of the couch. Autumn mentally measured the distance between the chair and where he sat on the couch. If she was going to share Kari's records with him, she'd have to sit on the couch next to him. Had Jon sat there on purpose or was she being silly? Autumn decided the last choice was correct. She picked up her iPad and sat next to Jon.

"What did Kelly tell you about Kari's pregnancy?"

"Not much. She said Kari was your patient and you'd fill

me in. I got the feeling that she didn't agree 100% with your assessment that Kari's risk factors required a doctor's care."

"Kelly thinks I'm being overly cautious. I had a mother last year who developed complications during the birth that could have been avoided if we'd been more cautious earlier in the pregnancy."

He nodded.

"But I haven't even gone over the details."

"My…I had an experience where earlier intervention and proper care would have made the difference between life and death."

"I'm so sorry. Did you lose the mother or the baby?"

"The mother died." His voice was flat. "It helped me decide to change my specialty from surgery to obstetrics."

"You weren't doing the delivery, then?" She spoke in a voice barely above a whisper.

"No." He cut the thread short with a shake of his head. "It's history. Tell me about Kari."

Autumn's heart went out to Jon for sharing a part of himself with her. To cover the show of sympathy she didn't think Jon would want, she tapped Kari's records open on the iPad and explained the situation.

"Unless I misunderstood, I thought you weren't doing deliveries."

"I'm not. Kari is more than a co-worker. She's a close friend and second cousin by her first marriage. When she and Eli found out they were pregnant, they asked me to do her prenatal care. I've known her since I was in high school. Her first husband, who was killed in Afghanistan, was a friend of Dad's. I want her to have the best care, not that I don't try to give all of my mothers the best care I can." She stopped. "As my grandmother would say, I'm running at the mouth. It's a problem I've had since kindergarten when I… No, you don't need to know that."

"I might like to." Jon's eyes were soft. "I imagine you were quite a lot like your sister, Sophie."

Autumn dropped her head and let her hair fall forward. She'd decided to leave it down. "Too much like Sophie. It must be Dad's influence. Now, as Gram would say, back on topic."

"I certainly will take Kari on."

"I'd hoped you would, but there's more. Kari is insisting that I continue to see her."

"You've lost me. I thought Kari had agreed to the referral."

"She has. She wants us to work together."

Jon jotted in his notebook. "I see. You'd be working under my supervision."

"No, more of a collaboration."

"Even better." He moved to the edge of the couch and leaned toward her.

A rush of relief and gladness ran through her. Jon didn't have to say yes, but he was more than agreeable. He wanted to work together.

"We can learn from each other. The more experiences you have, the better prepared you are for any complications that might arise."

She wasn't looking for complications. That was the purpose behind referring Kari to Jon, to avoid complications.

"I'd like to take a closer look at Kari's records and your notes before I see her."

"I had her sign the release before she and Eli left on vacation."

"Great. Have her call or stop in to make an appointment." He closed his notebook. "We can celebrate our collaboration with Nana's tarts or go out for soft-serve ice cream."

Autumn sat up straighter. "Let's save the ice cream celebration until after you talk with Kari. She and Eli have a definite birth plan they'll expect you to stick to. Eli is a retired Air Force Lieutenant Colonel, used to giving orders. And I have to warn you Kari knows too much about pregnancy and obstetrics. She's not an easy patient, and that's coming from a close friend."

"With you collaborating, I'm sure Kari and I will get along fine." Jon's lips curled up in the famous Hanlon smile.

If he used that smile on Kari enough times, they probably would. It was almost starting to get to her.

CHAPTER 11

"Welcome back from vacation," Autumn greeted Kari when she ran into her at the Grand Union grocery store in Schroon Lake.

"It's good to be back, if only to get a little rest and relief from the heat. Do you know what Washington in late July is like? No wonder we got such a good deal on the vacation package. Then the kids each wanted to do different things first, Eli included."

Kari paid for her groceries and Autumn pushed her cart up to the register and started unloading. "You didn't have a good time?"

"No, we had a lot of fun. Eli got everyone in line, and I took it easy." Kari made a face. "Eli threatened to rent me one of those scooters if I didn't. I watched what I ate, got in my recommended exercise in the morning and lounged around in the afternoons, letting the others do their own thing. I haven't been this caught up on my reading in years. I made everyone do their own unpacking and laundry when we got home."

"Good work."

Kari rested her hand on her baby bump. "Do you have some time to go talk somewhere?" Her gaze flickered to the teenage cashier and the woman behind Autumn."

"Sure. I'm free until two. The trivia group changed our bi-weekly social to this afternoon since Tessa has someone to cover the Saturday matinee this weekend but not the Sunday one."

"How's the group going? Any new members?" Kari asked. "I keep meaning to get back into it."

"Pretty well, and not really. Josh is working on a couple of the guys he works with." Autumn helped the bagger pack the last of her things. "How does the soft-serve stand sound, one of the outside tables?"

"Fine. What are we celebrating?"

Autumn groaned. Her father must have shared the family tradition with Kari, or maybe she had.

"We're celebrating your return from vacation. Kelly has been particularly difficult the past couple of weeks. I think her daughter Stephanie going away to college is bothering her."

They pushed their carts out into the parking lot.

"You're too kind. Some days I wonder why you stay with her. You've got the credentials, the experience, you could go somewhere else."

"I could ask you the same."

"Do that when we get to the soft-serve stand."

They went their separate ways to their cars. After they got their orders, Autumn and Kari sat at a shaded picnic table away from the other patrons.

"Mmmm." Kari relished a spoonful of chocolate ice cream. "See how good I am, I only got one scoop, not two, and no cone."

"A paragon of pregnant mothers, for sure." Autumn looked at her double scoop cone and thought about all of the baked goods Mrs. Hanlon had brought her the past weeks.

"Now, ask me again," Kari said.

"Ask you what?"

"Why I stay with Kelly."

"Okay, why?"

"I'm waiting to see what you do when your contract with Kelly is up in the fall."

Her contract. It was always in the back of her mind. As a midwife who didn't deliver babies, she didn't have many options open to her within commuting distance of Paradox Lake, unless she took a delivery nurse job at Adirondack Medical Center in Saranac Lake. Gratitude toward her friend filled her. "You can't know how much that means to me, but you should do whatever's best for you and your family."

"I hear one of the birthing center staff nurses may be leaving," Kari said.

"Signing on with the center would mean working with Dr. Hanlon." Autumn wasn't sure why she'd said that as if she were warning Kari. So far, she hadn't had any problem working with him.

"The scenery would be nice," Kari said.

It looked like Jon had added Kari to his list of admirers. "Speaking of Dr. Hanlon, be prepared to redo the glucose test and have another ultrasound. The orders are in your records."

"What's with that?" As if to challenge the orders, Kari jammed her spoon into the last bit of ice cream left in the dish. "My blood sugar counts since your last test have been within the acceptable range. Why redo them?"

"Give Jon some slack. It's his way. He likes to have his own tests and his own notes. He was concerned about a birth he covered for Maureen while she was on vacation. He felt he didn't have enough background on the pregnancy. I'm not surprised he wants to get as much as he can get on you."

"That doesn't bother you? It's like he's questioning what you've already done."

Autumn stopped mid-lick. Surprisingly, it didn't bother her. "No. We're not in a competition. We're collaborating. If Jon feels he needs additional tests, that's his call."

"Very interesting. I've seen you make far less than this into a competition."

Autumn looked over her cone at her friend, choosing to ignore that comment. "The additional tests. They're not a problem with your insurer, are they?"

"No, Eli has good coverage through the school. Now, back to your non-competition pact with Dr. Hanlon. Does that mean you're softening toward him?"

"I didn't realize I was hardened against him."

"Come on, you weren't thrilled when you found out he was the new center director."

"We had some history I needed to get past."

"And you have?"

She had. "I'll admit that if I'd first met Jon this summer, we'd get along fine." For whatever reason, his grandmother's words came back to her. *What he really needs is some happy normal births so he can see the real joy of new life. Birth isn't an enemy that has to be conquered.* "We are getting along fine, for that matter."

"Do I detect a maybe better than fine?"

Autumn shifted on the hard picnic table bench to get more comfortable. "No, you detect two colleagues, friends, getting along fine."

"Fine enough to join him?"

"Aren't you full of questions today. Is that what we get for letting you take vacation? If by joining him, you mean dating him, no not that fine. Not that he's asked." *Since we were at Samaritan, that is.* "And don't ask if that's a possibility."

"I won't, not today. What I mean is join him at the center. The scuttlebutt is that Adirondack Medical Center is shopping the birthing center as a comprehensive women's health center, based on your gynecological care and Dr. Craven's satellite office here."

"That's a stretch." Autumn snapped a bite of the cone off.

"Agreed. But you might want to stretch it to your advantage by talking to Dr. Hanlon about your joining the staff as a woman's clinician, if you're serious about not doing births anymore. Except mine." Kari smirked.

Adirondack Medical Center was shopping the birthing center? Jon just happened to be chosen director. His grandmother shows up for an extended visit. The sugar cone tasted dry in her mouth. In Autumn's head, it was all adding up to one thing. JMH Health Care, Jon's grandfather's company, taking over. She'd heard and read enough about his takeovers to know that a post-takeover birthing center wouldn't be somewhere she'd want to work.

"Yoo-hoo, you still with me?"

Autumn wrapped what was left of her cone in a napkin to toss it in the garbage. "Yes. I'll think about what you've said." After she asked her friend Jon a few questions.

THE ATTENDANCE at the trivia group's second social buoyed Jon's spirits about the trivia group. All of the regulars had come, along with several guests who seemed interested in joining them. Autumn's arriving early and asking if she could talk with him afterwards had added to the buoyant feeling.

He finished walking Josh and Lexi, the last of the group

members, to the door. "Bye." Jon pushed the screen door shut and joined Autumn. "Alone at last." He waited for her to respond to his tease with an exasperated smile and got a frown instead.

She perched on the edge of the chair. "I'll get right to the point. Did you take the position as director of the birthing center to help your grandfather take it over?"

"Never." He pushed himself from the seat he'd just taken and paced the length of the couch. "Who told you that?"

"No one in particular. I'm just connecting the dots. I heard that the medical center might be putting the birthing center on the market. It hasn't met financial expectations."

Jon knew it hadn't. That had been part of the challenge of taking the job. "I haven't heard anything official about selling the center." It didn't sit well with him to have the center staff speculating.

"Let me finish. You take over the birthing center. Your grandmother appears for an apparently unending stay. Today, Tessa said your grandmother had contacted her friend's real estate firm to view some high-end vacation properties, preferably ones that have been winterized."

"Nana did what?" He banged the back of the couch with the palm of his hand.

"She contacted a local realtor—"

He cut her off with a slice of his hand. "I heard that. I'm working on deciphering it." He dropped back into the chair. "Let me set you and the rest of Paradox Lake and Ticonderoga straight. I have nothing to do with my grandfather's business. I try to have nothing to do with him at all."

"Your grandfather owns JMH. Your father sits on the board. You're telling me that you have no interest at all in the family corporation?" Autumn's eyes flashed her challenge.

Jon's heart pounded with anger. "I'm telling you exactly that. According to what I've been told repeatedly since I chose not to follow the family footprints and practice surgery, I've essentially been disinherited by both my grandfather and father."

Autumn knitted her brow and tilted her head. "Seriously?"

He threw his hands up. "Who knows? That's what they both told me when I chose an obstetrics residency and made it clear I wasn't choosing it for the surgical opportunities. They could have almost accepted my choice if I'd gone into it for surgery."

Autumn pushed back into the chair and crossed her legs at the ankles. She cocked her head and one side of her mouth twisted up.

"If you're trying to figure out my crazy family, give up. I did a long time ago."

"I had to ask." Autumn's voice was barely above a whisper. "The birthing center is my and a lot of other people's livelihood. I've read what JMH does when it buys a facility, and a couple of the nurses at Samaritan had come from small Upstate hospitals that your grandfather had taken over. I couldn't, wouldn't, work in those conditions."

But if that happened, Autumn's family would be behind her, help her. Unlike his. He swallowed the bitter taste in his mouth. "Yes, I know what my illustrious grandfather does. He guts the heart of a facility and turns a profit on the backs of the staff and patients."

He shouldn't have, but he took satisfaction in Autumn's stunned silence. His grandfather had better not have plans to buy the Ticonderoga Birthing Center. That could interfere with his plans to bolster his vitae by saving the center himself. Disgust filled him. That sounded like something his father would say. It had to be his anger. He never put business and his own gain ahead of giving the people he served the best medical care he could. He'd taken the director position to improve his ability to provide care. So he'd have the administrative know-how he'd need to follow his calling to Haiti next year.

"So you're telling me that you don't know anything about your grandfather staging a takeover?"

"That's right."

"I'm glad to hear that."

Did he detect skepticism in her voice? No. From what he knew of Autumn, if she'd doubted his words, she'd say so. "I'll see what I can find out from Nana."

"I'd appreciate that."

"I can't guarantee anything. I can't even get her to tell me how long she's staying with me."

Autumn stood. "I'd better get going or I'll be late for dinner.

She had a dinner date? His stomach sank. He shouldn't be surprised. It was Saturday night.

"Gram hates when anyone is late."

A smile tugged at the corners of his lips. He couldn't think of any reason she'd tell him that except to break the tension. "And I know how important it is to keep grand-mothers happy." Jon paused waiting for Autumn's comeback. All he got was a nod and a "bye." But Autumn always had been one woman he hadn't been able to charm. Nana was another.

Jon stood at his door and watched Autumn walk to her side of the duplex. So, Autumn's Saturday night dinner date was with her grandparents. If that was typical of her social life, it rivaled his. Not that he'd been making any real effort to have a social life beyond the trivia group since he'd arrived in Paradox Lake, nor did he plan to. So, why was he so pleased Autumn's dinner date was with her grandparents?

He whistled Forever Wild's latest song as he made his way through the kitchen and out the back door to track

Nana down. She was right where he expected he'd find her, on the patio reading.

"Are your friends all gone?"

"Yes, Autumn was the last. She just left."

"You didn't ask her if she wanted to come over for dinner, did you? I want her to try out the lemon meringue pie. It's a new recipe."

"No, she said she had other plans. It is Saturday night and she's an attractive woman." Both statements were true and might help discourage Nana from her campaign to push them together. It was getting embarrassing and hard to resist.

"That's too bad. I really enjoy Autumn's company, don't you?"

"Yes, as a colleague and friend."

His grandmother smiled a knowing smile that he had to admit to himself wasn't too far off target.

Let her think what she wanted. He had more important things than his nonexistent love life to discuss with her. "Could you come inside? I have something I want to talk to you about."

"Something unpleasant from the look on your face."

"It doesn't have to be."

"That's cryptic." As they crossed the yard to the back door, his grandmother gestured toward the pines separating the duplex from the lake. "It really is beautiful here. Have you thought about buying some property, a house or land to build a house on?"

"No, although I hear you've been looking." He opened the door and followed his grandmother in.

"I have," she said, not elaborating. "Can I start dinner while we talk?"

"I'd rather have your full attention."

"That serious." She pulled out a chair and sat at the table.

He sat across from her, leaning on his elbows. "Is grandfather thinking about buying the Ticonderoga Birthing Center?"

Nana touched a finger to her cheek. "No, not that I'm aware. I haven't talked with him in weeks, but the facilities he was looking at then were mid-state and down near Binghamton. Where did you get the idea he was interested in your center?"

Nana's reference to the center as his bothered him. His work here was a stepping stone. He didn't want to take virtual ownership, like Autumn and many of the hometown staff seemed to. It would be easier to leave when the time came if he didn't. But he could still care about the center, care about keeping it open for Autumn and the others.

"Autumn asked. She said she'd heard that the Adirondack Medical Center might want to spin off the birthing center and insinuated that I might be part of a takeover plan instigated by Grandfather. Her points: my taking the directorship, your apparently unending stay, and the fact that you were shopping real estate here."

"I take it Autumn didn't like that idea."

"What do you think?"

"I wouldn't if I were her. So, I doubt she would, although a JMH takeover could keep the center open if it's in danger of closing. Autumn seems attached to living here, not that I blame her."

"Grandfather would destroy the center, like he destroys everything he touches."

"Jonathan," she admonished him. "He is your grandfather."

"And your husband." Jon crossed his arms across his chest. "Sorry."

"Apology accepted." Her eyes went soft. "You didn't know

him before when he was still practicing surgery. He was different."

Jon's chest tightened. He did remember loving to go to Nana and Grandfather's house when he was small.

She cleared her throat. "You can tell Autumn that I don't know anything about JMH taking over the birthing center."

"I will." Her words should have relieved the knot in his stomach, but they didn't. Nana wouldn't lie to him, but he had a niggling feeling she wasn't telling him something.

His grandmother stood, went to the refrigerator, and took a package of meat out of the freezer. "I thought I'd make lamb chops."

They were one of his favorites.

"With asparagus and baked potatoes."

"And mint jelly?" he asked.

"You've got it." She unwrapped the chops and put them in the microwave to defrost. "After dinner I'd like you to come with me to see the lake house I looked at yesterday. You can meet my realtor."

Jon drummed his fingers on the table. She thought she'd bribe him into coming with her by making his favorite foods. He stopped and laid his hand flat on the table. Grandfather was the schemer, not Nana. She'd probably planned this dinner days ago.

"I'd like to get a second opinion before I buy it," she said.

"You're that serious."

"I am. I might as well use the money my parents left me for something. I let your grandfather invest it and he tied it up in long-term investments to discourage me from spending it. He could take care of me just fine, thank you, is his way. My inheritance is where the money I sent you when you were in medical school came from."

Nana had money from her parents? He'd had no idea.

Even if it hadn't been a lot to begin with, if it had been invested all of those years, it could be a nice amount now.

"If, and that's a big if, your grandfather ever comes to his senses, it would make a great vacation home. And if he doesn't, it's completely winterized. I can't go on living here with you forever, not that I'm not enjoying myself."

"Sure, I'll go with you."

"I think you'll like it, and I know I'll like living near you, even if it turns out to be only during the summer. The house not only has a beautiful view, but it has an elaborate wooden jungle gym for kids to play on. Autumn said Paradox Lake was a great place to grow up."

Only he wouldn't be here past next year, and he certainly didn't have any immediate plans to provide Nana with any great grandkids to play on the jungle gym.

JON WAS STILL REHASHING his conversation with Nana as he left his place for work the next morning.

"Good morning." Autumn startled him. She usually left for the center later then him.

"'Morning."

"Do you have a minute? I'd rather talk here than at work."

"Sure." There was no actual requirement that he had to be the first one in.

"I wondered if you had a chance to talk with your grandmother."

"Yes." He certainly had.

"And," Autumn prompted him. "What did she say?"

Jon rubbed the back of his neck. "As far as Nana knows, Grandfather has no intention of buying the birthing center. But she did say they haven't talked in several weeks."

Autumn frowned.

He shrugged. "That's all I got." He hadn't had to add the part about Nana and Grandfather not communicating, and he wasn't going to share his unfounded feeling that Nana had held something back.

Autumn touched his arm as he started toward his bike. "I have something else to ask you. From what I heard the other day, Adirondack Medical Center is shopping the birthing center as a complete women's health center, based partly on my branching out more into gynecology."

He wasn't following Autumn's train of thought. "I don't know anything about that."

"Okay, but if it turns out to be right and there's an opening on staff for an OB/GYN nurse practitioner, I might be interested. My contract with Kelly is up soon."

Autumn wanted to join him on staff. The sun moved out from behind a cloud that had passed in front of it while they were talking with Kelly. So far, they'd worked well together, and he'd like having another practitioner on staff. "The minute I hear anything, I'll let you know. Or are you asking me to request the position? I'm willing to research the need and propose it if the numbers indicate a gap in service."

"Whoa, slow down. I'm just starting to consider alternatives to entering another contract with Kelly."

He gritted his teeth. He had rather irrationally jumped right on that. But a staff position would mean Autumn could stay in Paradox Lake, something he was sure she wanted to do. And he'd like to help her. She was a definite asset to the center and the community.

"Let's see how it goes working together with Kari. She said she scheduled her appointment with you."

"Yes, she has an appointment this week." He didn't want to tell her an appointment this Tuesday at three-thirty because she wouldn't believe he routinely remembered the dates and times of all his patients' appointments. He didn't.

"I can let you know tomorrow when it is if you want to sit in."

"No, why don't you see her alone this time and we can talk afterwards. Having both of us there might make Kari nervous that we're more concerned about her pregnancy than we, or at least I, am."

"True. I wouldn't want to alarm her." Insights like that were one of the reasons he thought they'd work well together overall, not only with Kari.

"I'd better get going. I have an early appointment," Autumn said.

Jon's gaze traced the delicate lines of her profile as she walked to her car. Autumn might have some reservations, but right now he couldn't think of anything he'd rather do than work with Autumn for as long as he was at the center.

CHAPTER 12

Sunday afternoon the sound of her cell phone drew Autumn away from the kitchen window where she'd been admiring Jon mowing the back lawn. He'd offered his services to her father, said he needed the exercise. One last look at his broad shoulders and trim waist belied that statement. But she welcomed not having to do the lawn herself, although considering all the dessert tasting Mrs. Hanlon had for her, she probably should volunteer to trade off with Jon.

She froze when she saw the birthing center contact service number on the caller ID. She wasn't supposed to be on the on-call list anymore, not since she'd stopped presiding at births. "Hello," she choked out.

"Autumn?"

"Yes."

The service employee identified herself. "I'm trying to reach Dr. Hanlon. He's not answering either one of his phones."

Autumn relaxed and leaned against the kitchen counter.

"I thought since you live next door, you could see if he's home and ask him to call me. If he's not, let me know."

"He's here." Autumn glanced out the window again. Jon was pushing the mower back toward the house. "He's out mowing the lawn. Hang on, I'll take the phone out to him." This was one of the times when living in a close-knit community where everyone knew everyone else's business was a good thing.

Jon reached the flowerbed next to Autumn's back door at the same time she opened the door. She waved her phone at him, and he turned the mower off. "It's your service."

He stepped over and took the phone from her, turning away to take the call. He handed it back when he was done. "I have to go. I'll finish the lawn during the week."

"One of your mothers?"

"No, actually, it's someone here on vacation. She's…"

Autumn understood when he stopped. Confidential information. "Don't worry about the grass. If I get ambitious, I'll pick up where you left off."

He sprinted over to his back door and went in. Her phone rang again. "Hi, Dad. What's up?"

"I'm glad I got you. You need to get over to the birthing center."

"What?"

"Christie Reynolds wants you there."

"You're not making sense."

"Christie's gone into labor early. She and her family are vacationing at the lake house her parents always rented when you were kids."

That Autumn knew, and she felt guilty that she hadn't gone over yet and visited with her. They'd been great friends the summers Christie's family had vacationed at Paradox Lake. She started to say she couldn't deliver Christie's baby, especially if it was premature, when she realized Jon's call must have been about Christie.

"Anne and I have her four-year-old with us. Your grandmother is driving her to the birthing center right now."

"So what did you need me for?" Even if she were still birthing babies, she would have called Jon in for a premature birth.

"Christie's husband isn't here. He wasn't coming to join them until Wednesday. Christie wants you there for moral support. She doesn't know Jon. She's pretty freaked."

"Got it. I'll let you know how things go. Bye." Autumn heard Jon's car start and hurried to the front door to see him speed off before she could get his attention.

Twenty minutes later, she entered the center. "Hi, Autumn," the woman at the front desk said. "They're waiting for you."

She went back into the birthing suites.

"Autumn, I'm so glad you're here." Christie pushed herself up in the bed. "She's coming too early."

"What happened?" Autumn glanced past Christie to Jon. Her head was full of questions she wanted to ask. But she didn't want to appear as if she were competing with him over Christie. He was the medical provider in charge.

Jon nodded, iPad in hand and his paper pad sticking out of his pants pocket. "We were just getting started."

"I've been having twinges the past couple of days. I didn't think they were contractions. I was going to call you yesterday, but I didn't have your number. I tried your dad, but no one was home and I decided I was being overly concerned. It's not my first baby. I thought they felt like the false labor I'd had with Connor. Then this morning my water broke. That's when I called your dad and your grandmother drove me in."

Autumn had been so focused on Christie that she hadn't even noticed her grandmother in the suite.

"The pains I'm having now aren't twinges."

"How often?" Autumn and Jon said in unison.

"Not often. I had one on the ride here and one while I was checking in. None since."

"When is your due date?" Autumn asked.

"Not for another four or five weeks. Connor came really fast. He surprised my doctor. Autumn, I'm scared."

Autumn squeezed her hand. She was, too. The center wasn't set up for high-risk babies. Christie's eyes pleaded with her for more assurance. Her friend Suzy had looked at her the same way when the complications arose during her baby's birth. At times like this, Autumn could see why some practitioners preferred not to treat people they were close to.

"How fast did your son come?"

Christie turned at Jon's question. "In about six hours. My doctor said that was quick for a first baby."

Jon's eyes narrowed. He was probably calculating the time needed to get Christie to either the Adirondack Medical Center hospital or Albany Medical Center. If it were her call, she'd choose Albany Med, even though Adirondack was an hour away and Albany was two. Albany had one of the largest and most sophisticated neonatal intensive care units in the East.

"Did you call your doctor?" Autumn asked.

"I talked to him before I called your dad. He asked me if I could get to the hospital in Albany. I told him my transportation situation and that I knew you, that you're a midwife here at the birthing center. His office called the birthing center."

"I talked with Christie's obstetrician while she was getting signed in and her vitals checked," Jon said.

So Jon already knew all the things she'd been asking Christie, except how fast her last birth was. The surprise on his face had been plain when Christie had said six hours.

"Her doctor wants us to have Christie transported to Albany. He's making the referral. Would you call the emergency services and arrange it? You can use the phone in my office. It's open."

Before Autumn could answer, Christie doubled over and wrapped her arms around her stomach.

Jon looked at his watch, obviously checking the time since her last contraction. He eyed the electronic fetal monitor.

Christie straightened. "I'm okay," she said before Autumn or Jon could ask.

"I'll be right back," Autumn said. She'd let Jon decide whether to put Christie on the monitor. This was his birth.

"I'll walk out with you," her grandmother said. "Christie, we'll all be thinking about you and the baby."

"Thank you, Mrs. Hazard."

Once they got into the hall, Autumn cracked. "Gram, what if something goes wrong, bad, like with Suzy? I couldn't handle that, not again."

Her grandmother hugged her. "You're not alone. You have Jon and the medical people in Albany to take over. That is, if you get her to Albany. Don't you have a call to make?"

Autumn pulled back from her grandmother's embrace. "Right, the ambulance service."

JON JOTTED a note in his pad while he waited for Autumn to return. Christie was on the phone with her husband, asking him to meet them at the Albany Medical Center. He glanced at the doorway. Where was she?

"Sorry I took so long." Autumn stood at the door motioning him out.

"What?" he asked, closing the suite door behind him.

"There's a big pile-up on the Northway. I couldn't get any ambulance service. Ticonderoga, Moriah, and Schroon Lake have all responded, so they're not available. Elizabethtown is on standby. They can't go to Albany."

He leaned his head against the wall and closed his eyes, running through his options. Letting anything happen to mother or baby wasn't among them. They could wait until transportation was available, calling in one of the local pediatricians if they had to deliver here. He and Autumn could drive Christie to Saranac Lake, where the facility was a little better equipped for a premature baby. Saranac could air transport to Albany later, if necessary. Or…He pushed away from the wall.

"We're going to have to transport Christie to Albany ourselves."

Autumn paled.

"It's our best choice. We can get there in two hours. She won't have the baby before then," he said with a certainty he didn't feel. Babies followed their own time schedule.

"I could try one of the emergency squads south of here. It would take them a while to get here, but they probably weren't called to the accident."

"No, the best plan is for us to take her. In your car. It's bigger. Do you have gas?"

"I filled up yesterday."

"We can do this. I'll get the equipment. You go tell Christie what we're doing. If it gets dicey, we can go to the Glens Falls hospital. Glens Falls is, what, about halfway to Albany?"

"Yes." Autumn pushed her hair behind her ears. "We could make Glens Falls."

"Of course we can." He paused. "That accident isn't on the south side of the Northway is it?"

"I don't know. I was so frustrated with none of the ambulances being available that I didn't ask." She swallowed her fear. If the route south was blocked, they could be in big trouble.

CHAPTER 13

*C*ars were backed up miles for the accident, which fortunately was on the north side of the Northway. Jon sped by them, acutely aware of Autumn and Christie talking in the back seat. Their words were punctuated every so often by a quiet groan or quick intake of breath by Christie. He timed the groans by the dashboard clock.

"Glens Falls is the next exit. How are we doing?"

"Fine," Christie said. "The contractions are sharper, but no closer together."

"I know, I've been timing them," Jon said.

Christie laughed. "So has Autumn."

He wasn't surprised. When it came to practicing obstetrics, he and Autumn had a lot in common. Maybe in other ways, too. But since he didn't plan to stay in the North Country, it wouldn't be fair to Autumn to find out, as much as he might want to.

"We're good for Albany, then?" Jon caught Christie nodding in the rearview mirror.

"All systems go," Autumn replied. "As long as the contractions don't start coming too fast."

Twenty minutes later, Christie let out a sharp, "Ouch." She gasped. "They're getting stronger."

Jon checked the clock. *And closer.*

"We're only a half hour, 40 minutes tops, away from Albany Med," Autumn said in a soothing voice. "Right Jon?"

"Right." He pressed the gas pedal harder and increased their speed another five miles an hour. The hint of a quiver he heard in Autumn's question had increased the pounding of his heart. He breathed deeply. He'd delivered premature babies before and hadn't lost one of them. They were minutes away from a state-of-the-art medical facility, not in rural Haiti. He cleared his throat. Angie always came first in his thoughts when he faced a challenging birth.

"Jon."

Autumn didn't have to finish her sentence. He saw the state police car with its flashing lights and pulled over.

"Officer." He handed over his license and car registration. "I'm Dr. Hanlon. We're transporting a woman in labor to Albany Med from the Ticonderoga Birthing Center. The local ambulances were all tied up with that accident on the Northway."

The officer looked in the back seat where Christie was gripping Autumn's hand with white knuckles as another contraction wracked her. "You should have called it in, Dr. Hanlon. Go ahead. You'll be good to the medical center." He waved them off, and Jon merged back into traffic.

"Autumn, call the medical center and let them know we'll be there within the half hour, so they'll be ready for Christie."

"They're on alert," she said after she clicked off the call.

When they arrived at Albany Med, a team from The Birth Place and Children's Hospital descended on them as they helped Christie into the facility. They had her on a gurney and whisked off before he'd finished talking with the attending physician Christie's doctor had referred her to.

That was close. Jon blew out a quick breath to regain his mental balance and returned to where Autumn was standing. "They're in good hands. Albany has a top-rated NICU."

Autumn clasped her hands, concern still etched in her face.

"She'll be fine," Jon reassured her.

"I'd like to stay until the baby is born. If you need to get back to Paradox Lake, I'll get a hotel room for the night."

"Of course we'll stay." Autumn had worked with him enough at Samaritan to know he always saw things through. A pang of old guilt pierced him. Work things. He hadn't been as conscientious with his social life. He'd tended to let people think what they chose to think rather than tying up any loose ends for them.

"Thanks for staying with me. I'm sure Christie's husband would let Dad know tomorrow when he came by for Connor. But I couldn't sleep tonight not knowing."

Part of Jon knew he should correct Autumn's assumption that he was staying for her. It was as much for him as for Autumn. The other part of him liked giving the impression that he cared enough for her to stay because she wanted him to. It was easier than putting how he was starting to feel about her in words she could reject. "I wouldn't be able to sleep either," he said.

Autumn's smile warmed him head to toe.

"I don't know about you, but I'm hungry. We could grab something in the cafeteria and eat it in The Birth Place waiting room," she said.

"Sound good to me. I'll treat."

"You don't have to."

"What if I want to?"

Several expressions chased each other across her face, all

of which warmed him further. "Then I'll let you," she conceded.

OVER THE NEXT FEW HOURS, Jon and Autumn paced the waiting room—sometimes solo, sometimes together—and hit the coffee machine in the hall for refills, which did nothing good for their growing tension.

Autumn checked her watch. "Didn't Christie say her labor was only six hours with Connor?"

Jon stopped mid pace. "Yeah. From my experience, this baby should have come faster, especially since it's early."

"*She's* early," Autumn said.

He ignored the edge to her correction. "I asked the attending to have someone let us know after the birth."

"And I told Christie I would stay. She said she'd have her husband come and tell us how the baby was."

They looked at each other, the wall clock ticking off another minute.

"It has to have been six hours or more since Christie went into labor," Autumn said. "I'll go make sure the nurses know we're here." She turned and left.

He dropped into the closest chair and held his head in his hands. The nursing shift would have changed since they'd arrived. If they were really busy today, the outgoing nurses could have forgotten to tell the incoming ones. He wanted to believe that was the case. The only other reason he could come up with was that there were complications prolonging the labor or—he swallowed—Christie's husband wasn't in any shape to come and talk with them.

A few minutes later, Jon sensed, rather than heard, Autumn return. He lifted his head.

"No baby yet," she said. "And they know we're here." She

raised her hands, which had an insulated paper cup in each. "I got us refills."

His stomach churned. He didn't think he could swallow another mouthful of coffee.

"It's not from the machine."

His face must have given his thoughts away.

"I got the good stuff, fresh brewed, from the nurses' lounge."

He accepted the cup and took a sip. "Not bad." While the brew was a lot better than the coffee from the machine, it still hit his stomach like a rock.

Autumn settled in the chair next to him and lifted her cup to her lips. "What?" she said when she lowered it.

"Pardon?"

"You were staring at me."

He dropped his gaze to the cup he held in both hands on his lap.

"You're as worried as I am, aren't you?" she asked.

Jon's first reaction was denial. Hanlon men didn't admit fear or second guess their decisions. But he *was* concerned. He'd expected the birth to go much faster. What had he missed? He'd gone over their actions several times while he was waiting for Autumn to return. "We could have had her airlifted here. But I didn't see a need."

"And the accident on the Northway would have had the priority on those services, as it did with the local ambulance services," Autumn said. "You're not infallible. You can't see everything."

But I'm supposed to be, or as close as possible. He lifted his head. Her light blue eyes shimmered with moisture. "What is it?" he asked.

"I had a mother who had a placenta percreta. The placenta had grown through her uterus. I didn't catch it during her prenatal care. The worst happened during the birth."

He swallowed, waiting for her to say she'd lost the mother.

"She can't have any more children."

"But she and the baby were okay."

She nodded. "They're close friends of mine." Her voice cracked. "We went to high school together. They wanted a houseful of kids. Now, they can't have that, and it's my fault." Her free hand gripped the armrest between them.

He covered her hand with his. "Is that why you've given up delivering babies?" he asked, second guessing himself again as he wondered whether he should have kept his question to himself. She looked so fragile. He didn't want to pressure her.

"Yes." Her answer was barely audible. "You're the only one I've told besides Kari and Kelly."

His breath caught. *Not even her family?*

"They saw me fail. I had to tell them."

But she didn't have to tell him. She'd chosen to. His heart swelled.

"During my next birth, I froze when the mother reached late-labor. I had to send Kari to get Kelly. It was awful." Autumn wiped tears from her cheeks with the palms of her hands. "Fortunately, it was at the center, and Kelly was in the office. I said I was ill and left. I can't take the responsibility, can't do it anymore."

Jon massaged her hand with his thumb. He wanted to tell her "yes you can." He'd seen her at work at the center, at Lisa Kent's delivery. But he knew no words could fix what was inside her. She'd have to do that herself.

The squeeze of her fingers calmed his jangled nerves, and they sat hands clasped until the sound of footsteps in the hall outside the room yanked them both from their reflective silence.

She jumped to her feet as a very tired-looking man entered the waiting room.

"Autumn?" he said.

"Yes." The word came out with a whoosh.

"Christie said you'd be here waiting. And Dr. Hanlon."

The man must be Christie's husband. Jon closed the space between him and Autumn in one stride and clamped his jaw shut to let the man speak at his own speed.

"How are they?" Autumn rolled forward and back on the balls of her feet as if she couldn't contain the pent-up energy that radiated from her.

The fatigue lines bracketing Christie's husband's mouth deepened. Jon tensed, wanting and fearing to hear his next words.

"They're both fine, except for the baby's nose. She came face up and her nose was pushed over. The doctor said they'd tape it in place, and it would be good as new tomorrow."

"How much does she weigh?" Jon asked. The nose was nothing. The doctor would have snapped the soft cartilage in place and that would be that.

"Five pounds, fourteen ounces. Nineteen inches long."

"That's good sized for a late pre-term baby," Jon said.

"The pediatrician said Christie's due date might have been off."

"The baby's lungs?" Autumn shot out.

"No apparent problems. She came out squalling loud and angry."

"I'm so glad," Autumn said. "Christie will be going home to Poughkeepsie?"

"Yes, as soon as the pediatrician releases the baby. Hopefully, by the end of the week."

"Ask Christie to give me a call me before she goes home. She has my number now."

"I will."

"And will we see you at the lake next summer?"

"Maybe even this fall for the vacation we missed out on this week, if the house is available."

"I'm sure that would be fine. Talk to Dad when you pick Connor up. I'll look forward to seeing you all then."

"I'm going to get back to Christie. They're setting me up to bunk in her room."

"Nice meeting you," Jon said. "Maybe I'll see you when you're up in the fall, too."

Christie's husband left the waiting room and Autumn turned to Jon. They stared at each other for a moment before Autumn threw her arms around him in a hug. Her relief fueled his in an electric charge that first held them in a motionless embrace and then pushed them apart with a force as strong as the one that had drawn them together.

"I'm so glad everything turned out as well as it did," she said, stepping back to widen the space between them.

He reached for her hands and held them in his. "Me, too." It had felt good to share his fears and relief, even if his words weren't actually saying that.

"Christie and the baby had to be okay. I couldn't be responsible for another friend's..." Her voice broke. "Tragedy."

The stark pain on her face tore his heart, so he did the only thing he could to relieve it. He pulled her hands and stepped toward her. Bending his head, he pressed his lips to hers to kiss her with all of the feelings that had been building inside him since that first evening when he'd toured the birthing center. When her grip on his hands relaxed, he lifted his head.

His heart ached to comfort her more. "You have to stop

blaming yourself. Sometimes things are out of our hands, no matter what our expertise. We can only do our best.

Autumn blinked at him in confusion.

He rushed on to explain what he'd never explained to anyone else, not even Nana when she'd supported his choice of medical specialty, although he suspected she had a good idea that he'd chosen obstetrics because of Angie. "My cousin Angie worked with an aid agency in Haiti. She had complications after she went into labor and there was no doctor to help. She couldn't get the care she needed."

"I'm so sorry," Autumn said.

"Thanks. Your birth wasn't like Angie's. She had no one who could help. Your friends had the best care possible, you."

"But I should have…"

"No shoulds," he interrupted.

A thoughtful look replaced some of the pain on her face. "Kari said that Suzy and Jack have applied to become foster parents."

He nodded in reassurance. "See? And your quick action got Christie to Albany Med for the care she and her baby needed."

"My action, along with your help."

Help that Jon longed to continue to give Autumn until she regained her faith in herself, until she could confidently go back to catching babies for the women in her hometown who needed those services.

Autumn's lips turned up in a weak smile that called him to taste their softness again. He pulled her into his arms and did just that.

When he released her, she smiled up at him. "We do work well together. In more ways than one," she said, restarting the double-time tattoo of his heart that had finally started to slow.

"We need to investigate those other ways."

"How do you propose we do that, Dr. Hanlon?"

"We might try putting our kissing into a more appropriate setting by going on a date."

He loved the way her cheeks pinked when he'd said "kissing."

"I do hear that's how other people do it."

He took her hands again. "Seriously, I care for you and want to see if whatever is going on between us is something real."

"Me, too." She rose on her toes and gave him a peck on the lips.

Her sweet response was almost enough to make him forget that a relationship with Autumn didn't fit into his plans right now.

AUTUMN HAD FALLEN asleep on the drive back from Albany with the taste of Jon's lips on hers and his admission that he reciprocated her feelings humming in her heart. They'd parted ways with another toe-curling kiss when they'd reached the duplex. Now, two days later, she still couldn't get Jon's kisses off her mind, although the anticipation of moving their relationship forward was waning. He'd yet to actually ask her out on a date.

She took extra care braiding her hair into a French braid and applying her makeup, telling herself that her particular attention to her appearance was because she and Kelly had a meeting with potential new parents after Kari's appointment and not because she'd be seeing Jon.

Enough! She dropped her mascara wand in her make-up bag. Who was she kidding? She wanted to look nice for Jon. He'd finally won her over. It hadn't been his movie star good looks or the killer smile that made other women swoon. It was getting to know him as a man who could be depended on, a man who wasn't the cad her former roommate had made him out to be, nor the player he was reputed to be at Samaritan. A caring man she could share her personal and professional life with if her future in Paradox Lake was more certain.

CHAPTER 14

"Whew!" Kari fanned herself as she and Autumn walked back to their office from Jon's after Kari's appointment. "What was that?"

"I don't know what you're talking about," Autumn said. After she'd told Jon that it would be better to see Kari the first time without her, Kari had insisted she come this time. Autumn couldn't very well tell Kari she didn't want to sit in on her appointment because Jon had kissed her, said he wanted to date her, and then hadn't asked her out. It was all too high schoolish.

"You, Jon. The electricity in the air. I was afraid it would short out all of the electronics in the room."

Autumn lifted her hand and placed it on Kari's forehead palm out.

"What are you doing?"

"Did Jon's nurse take your temperature?"

"Ye-es." Kari drew out her answer.

"I was checking to see if you have a fever that's making you delirious."

"I'm not delirious. Admit it. There's something sparking between you two."

Autumn bit back the "there is not" that leapt to her tongue. She didn't want to sound like she was protesting too much. "Jon and I shared a harrowing birth on Sunday. My childhood friend Christie was vacationing at the house Dad rents out at the lake. Her baby wasn't due for five more weeks, but her water broke and the baby was coming fast. We had to transport her to Albany Med. Everything turned out fine, but the experience brought us together." Autumn touched her finger to her lips.

"It's about time," Kari said.

Autumn ignored her comment and pushed the door to their office open.

Lexi looked up from the computer. "Jon called. You forgot your meeting with him."

"Our meeting? I just came from Kari's appointment with him." Autumn looked at Kari, who grinned back at her.

"I don't know." Lexi shrugged. "He sounded like he was expecting you. I said I'd send you right down," she prompted when Autumn made no effort to leave.

Send her down? If he'd wanted her to stay, he could have said something. As Autumn turned to leave, she heard a stifled giggle from Lexi followed by "shush" from Kari. Were Jon and them up to something? Her heartbeat quickened along with her steps. *No.* She stopped herself. He'd probably assumed she'd stay to go over Kari's appointment, and her friends were making more of it than there was.

Jon met her in the hall outside of his office and opened the door so they could enter.

"We can talk here." He motioned to the couch in the waiting area.

Autumn sat. "Are you going to get your notes? I assume you want to talk about Kari."

"No, this is personal." He made himself comfortable on the couch next to her; the clean crisp smell of his after shave emphasized his nearness.

Autumn clasped her hands in her lap. Was this where he said he didn't want to see her after all? That his admission Sunday evening had been a let-down reaction to the tension of Christie's emergency delivery?

"I finished my research on the center's need for a gynecological nurse practitioner on staff and sent the request to HR."

That's what he'd wanted to tell her? How was that personal?

When she didn't respond, he added, "I recommended you for the position, assuming it's approved." He leaned back in the couch, a Cheshire Cat smile on his face.

Nothing about their kiss or date or relationship? "Thank you," she got out.

"Stunned you, didn't I?"

"Yes, yes you did." Stunned was right. If Jon's request went through, her job situation here would be a lot more secure. And it could mean the birthing center's financial situation was better than the center grapevine thought. In which case, she should be feeling more than stunned. Or it could mean the medical center was finessing appearances for a sale.

"I'll let you know as soon as I hear anything from HR."

"Please do."

"And, now…"

The office door opened, and Kari and Lexi wheeled in a utility cart with a luncheon for two.

"I wanted to take you out to lunch," he said, "but didn't have enough time between appointments, so I ordered in."

So that's what Lexi's giggle had been about. "My favorite.

Seafood Cobb Salad from the Corner Café. How did you know?"

Jon nodded toward Kari, who was slipping out the door behind Lexi.

"I should have known."

He placed their meals and two glasses of iced tea on the table in front of the couch. "Surprised?"

"Yes." And pleased at the pains he'd taken to surprise her.

"I knew telling you about the staff position would throw you off."

"You did that with your message to Lexi about our meeting I knew we didn't have."

He leaned back and gave her the famous Hanlon smile. Today it seemed different, more intimate, and went right to her core, melting her from the inside out.

Jon dug into his salad, giving her time to recompose herself.

"This is really good," he said. "It's not something I'd normally order. I tried it because Kari said you loved it."

Autumn almost choked on her shrimp. "Isn't that laying it on a little thick? The lunch is enough for me."

He shrugged and grinned. They talked about nothing and everything while they finished their lunch.

"Before we have to get back to work," he said, would you like to take a cruise of Lake George some evening next week? It would give us an opportunity to broaden our kissing horizons beyond medical facilities."

"When you put it that way, how can I refuse?" Autumn had been on various cruises of Lake George. None of them had had the appeal or promise of Jon's invitation.

"I'll see what night I can get tickets for and let you know." His office phone rang. "Excuse me." He walked to his desk and picked it up. "Yes, we just finished." He hung up and turned to her. "My next appointment is here."

As if on cue, Kari and Lexi reappeared and swept the lunch dishes away.

"I'll let you know about the cruise and see you Sunday."

"Sounds good."

As she headed back to her office, it struck her that today was only Tuesday. He'd said he'd see her Sunday. Maybe he was taking some time off. But why wouldn't he have mentioned it to her?

So THAT'S why Jon had said he'd see her Sunday. She slapped her copy of the *TiTimes* against her leg as she stomped over to his place to give him a good piece of her mind. While she'd been acting like a high schooler, all jazzed about the Lake George cruise, and daydreaming about her and Jon working together to make the birthing center a premier facility, he'd been destroying that possibility. This was the same man who'd said he'd broken up with her former room-mate because Kate hadn't been straight with him?

"Hi, you're just in time to sample my crullers," Mrs. Hanlon said when she opened the door. "I made them for coffee hour at church tomorrow."

"No thanks. I need to talk to Jon."

Mrs. Hanlon ushered her in. "He's not here. Didn't he tell you?"

"No, he didn't." She dropped the newspaper open on the coffee table.

"I'm sure he meant to. He's had a lot on his mind."

She eyed the newspaper on the table. *I'm sure he has.*

Mrs. Hanlon pulled the door closed. "He's been gone the past three days on his annual birthday canoeing trip in the Catskill Mountains with a couple of his college friends and my grandson-in-law, Angie's husband."

Apparently there were a lot of things he hadn't told her.

"He didn't mention it to me. Nor did he say anything about this." She pointed at the front-page story in the *Times*.

"Adirondack Medical Center To Sell Ticonderoga Birthing Center"

"It's to your husband's company."

Rather than the surprise Autumn expected to see from Mrs. Hanlon, the woman dropped her gaze to the newspaper, then picked it up and skimmed the article.

She folded the paper and put it back on the table. "The article says the sale isn't finalized."

"It says it's being finalized." Mrs. Hanlon's hair-splitting made Autumn's heart sink. She couldn't believe the woman would have lied to Jon about not knowing anything about any sale of the birthing center. But her demeanor indicated she knew something now. Autumn's thoughts jumped from Mrs. Hanlon to Jon. What did he know?

"Would that be so bad, the center being spun off?" Mrs. Hanlon asked, twisting her diamond ring back and forth on her finger.

"No offense. But your husband's business model isn't one I could work under." And, from what Jon had said to her, she'd thought he couldn't either.

"No offense taken. I don't agree with the direction my Jon has taken the company."

Mrs. Hanlon got a far-away look in her eyes. "He was different, more like Jay, your Jon, when he was practicing surgery."

Autumn ignored the possessive Mrs. Hanlon had put on Jon. *The way he's acting, he's not my anything*, she thought, her heart shrinking in her chest.

"My Jon once took great satisfaction in helping people and started JMH to help keep medical facilities open in areas where there are health professional shortages. He surprised me by curtailing his surgery practice to devote time to JMH. He loved surgery."

Autumn didn't know why Mrs. Hanlon was telling her all of this. She wanted to cut to the chase and find out when Jon would be home. But she wasn't about to interrupt. Mrs. Hanlon seemed to need to talk.

"He became bitter when the arthritis forced him to stop practicing. He was too young. Not ready to retire. He tried to hide it, but his partners noticed. After they asked him to step down from doing surgical procedures, he poured all of his bitterness into making money, with JMH as his money-making vehicle." Mrs. Hanlon wrung her hands. "What am I doing, dumping all of this on you?"

"It's okay." Autumn put her arm around the older woman. She couldn't say that she felt any warmer toward Jon's grandfather or JMH as it was now. But she could sympathize with Mrs. Hanlon and wondered how much, if any, of this Jon knew. From his outburst when she'd asked him about JMH buying the birthing center, she knew he'd disagree with his grandmother that he and his grandfather were anything alike. Or—she eyed the newspaper—could that outburst have been staged for her? She didn't want to believe that.

Mrs. Hanlon caught her gaze when she raised it from the newspaper. "You did read that the sale isn't entirely to JMH."

"Would your husband and JMH take a minority interest?" Autumn shook her head. "I have trouble believing that. It goes against his and the corporation's cutthroat reputation."

Hurt passed over the older woman's face.

"Sorry," Autumn said. "I'm upset, although that doesn't excuse me."

The older woman rubbed her temples. "I'm starting to get a headache. It must have been the heat from the deep fryer."

Or the way she'd stormed in and insulted the woman's

husband. "Sit down." Autumn stepped to the side so Mrs. Hanlon had access to the couch. "Can I get you aspirin?"

"No, I'll get it and go lie down for a while. That is if you can pick Jon up at the train station for me."

Talking to Jon had been her purpose for coming over here. But uncertainty about his knowledge of, and possible role in, the sale of the birthing center made a part of her rebel against being trapped in a car with him for the half-hour drive home. Since she'd let down her barriers against falling for him, it could be too painful.

Mrs. Hanlon's pale complexion quelled the rebellion. Autumn couldn't let the older woman drive if she was unwell. She was a big girl. She could get past her disappointment. "Of course. Will you be all right until we get back? I can call Gram, and I'm sure she'd come and stay with you."

"I'll be fine." She checked her watch. "Jon's train is due in a half hour. I'll call and let him know you're on your way."

"Okay." Autumn picked up the newspaper. She'd almost told Mrs. Hanlon not to call, to let her surprise Jon. On second thought, though, whether he was part of the birthing center sale or not, telling him she'd found out about it would probably be enough of a surprise.

JON DIDN'T KNOW what was wrong with him. He always looked forward to the guys' annual canoe trip and had been disappointed that he could only take three days off for it this year. The weather had been fabulous, the company good, and the food great. What more could a guy want? He looked out of the train window, but instead of the mountain scenery, he saw Autumn looking up at him, her eyes bright with the relief that Christie and her baby were fine.

If only they'd reconnected two years from now, after his

service in Haiti was complete and he'd done his part to make sure his cousin's death wasn't in vain. Would Autumn understand why he had to leave the birthing center when his contract was up next year? Could they build something between now and then that would be strong enough for him to ask her to wait for him to return?

The train pulled into the Ticonderoga stop and Jon made his way to the door, the only passenger getting off. He looked around the small waiting area for Nana. When he didn't see her, he sat on the wooden bench and checked his cell phone. *No service*. The station door opened a couple of minutes later, and Autumn, not Nana, walked in. He grabbed his duffle bag and met her mid-way across the room. Autumn's thin-lipped expression raised hairs on his neck. "Where's Nana? Is she okay?"

"I think so. She has a headache and wanted to rest so she asked me to pick you up. Didn't she call you?"

"She did and left a voicemail. When I tried to check it, I had no service. Did you take her temperature?"

"No, I took her at her word that all she needed was some rest. It's hot and she'd been cooking crullers in the deep fryer."

The short way Autumn answered troubled him, as if there might be a reason Autumn wouldn't take her word. Nana hadn't been feeling well earlier in the week but had told him it was fine for him to go on his trip.

"Thanks for looking after her." He pushed the door open with his shoulder and let Autumn go out ahead of him. Whenever he thought he'd adjusted to Nana living with him, something like this would happen that would throw him off. How many minor illnesses had Nana had over the years that he knew nothing about? He'd never given it a thought. Living in close proximity of someone you cared for who also cared for you was new to him. He liked it, even if it was sometimes trying.

Jon glanced over the car at Autumn. He was beginning to understand her attachment to Paradox Lake and living near her family and friends. It was nice having Nana with him, and he'd miss her when she left or—he thought of the lake house she was buying—when he left for Haiti.

He picked up the newspaper that was on the passenger side seat and slid into the car.

"It's this week's *TiTimes*," Autumn said. "Look at the lead story. They've scooped the Glens Falls daily."

Jon turned the paper over in his lap and read the headline, "Adirondack Medical Center To Sell Ticonderoga Birthing Center." He slammed his hand on the dashboard. "He wouldn't!"

"You didn't know about this?" Skepticism laced her question.

He rolled the newspaper into a tube and rapped it against his leg. The pain he'd felt when he'd broken his ankle playing basketball in high school couldn't hold a candle to the pain caused by Autumn's accusation that he'd lied to her when she'd asked before about JMH buying the birthing center.

"No, I didn't know anything about Grandfather buying the birthing center when you asked me before, and I don't know anything now."

"And you're not one of the consortium of private investors who's buying it with your grandfather?"

"Ha!" His laugh was bitter. She should know he didn't have that kind of money. He'd told her so. And while Autumn might be angry with him, he was equally angry. Only his anger was directed 100% at the proper target. His grandfather.

"No, I'm not one of the private investors. Can I call a truce here? I'm as much in the dark about this as you are."

One thing he did know was he wasn't going to let his grand-father kill what was between him and Autumn before it even had a chance to get started.

Autumn's shoulders slumped. "Sorry. That was harsh. I jumped to what I thought was the obvious conclusion. When you told me Tuesday that you'd recommend me for the new staff position if it's approved, it was the answer to my job prayers. Then I read that." She poked a finger at the rolled newspaper. "I took my disappointment out on you. I can't work for your grandfather, even if the staff job is still a possibility."

"I know." The air conditioner ruffled a strand of hair at her temple that had worked loose from her braid. He lifted his hand and smoothed it back behind her ear. She turned her cheek into his palm, her skin soft against his. This could solve the problem of their impending separation. If Autumn didn't have a job at the birthing center, she might come with him to Haiti. His heart lightened. Grandfather could be doing him a favor.

Autumn pulled up in front of the duplex and turned off the car.

"I'm going to get a hold of Grandfather and see what details I can find out," Jon said. If his grandfather would even talk to him after he'd ignored his order to send Nana home. "Since the medical center hasn't given me any official notif-ication, I figure the deal is still in negotiations and, in that case, I'm not likely to learn much."

"You'll let me know? The news article doesn't say how much of an interest the other partners have." Autumn looked at him in expectation.

He longed to reassure her. But he couldn't imagine Grandfather going into business with anyone but like-minded dollar-first people. "I'll share what I learn, officially and unofficially. And Adirondack Medical Center will have to issue some kind of statement to employees now that news of the sale is out."

"True. I'd better get in." She opened the door. "I'm catching a movie tonight with Lexi."

"What, no Josh? I thought he and Lexi were inseparable." He was stalling to keep Autumn with him and put off his call to his grandfather. He had no real interest in Josh and Lexi's dating.

"Josh's high school girlfriend has returned to Paradox Lake, and he wants to see her, too. Since Lexi is most likely here only for the summer, they've decided to cool it some. I thought I'd take Lexi out to cheer her up. Tessa is going to join us afterwards."

Jon felt sorry for Lexi, even though there was a time not too long ago when he'd dated a different woman every few months and, at times, more than one woman and hadn't thought anything of it. He looked back at his former actions with distaste.

They got out of the car. He slipped her hand in his and walked her to her door. "I'll let you know what I find out," he said again, squeezing her hand and releasing it before he trudged over to his side of the duplex.

He didn't get Nana's usual cheerful "hello" when he entered the house. She must still be resting. That left him nothing to do except make his phone call. He punched in Grandfather's number and paced the living room while the phone rang. He stayed out of his grandfather's life. Why couldn't Grandfather stay out of his? Finally, at the point where Jon expected the call to go to voicemail, his grandfather picked up.

"Grandfather, it's Jon."

"Jay," his grandfather said. "I've been expecting to hear from you."

Jon gritted his teeth at his grandfather's intentional use of the nickname he'd dropped years ago. "I want the details. All of them. What are you doing with my birthing center?"

"Making it yours. But I'm the silent partner on this deal. If you want details, you're going to have to talk with your grandmother." His grandfather clicked off.

CHAPTER 15

*J*on pulled his bike into the parking space on his side of the duplex. His ride had done little to blow off his anger at his grandfather for hanging up on him or help him puzzle out what was going on. He'd gotten as far as figuring out Nana must be one of the private investors. But why? Grandfather had to be behind her investment. Maybe JMH was having credit problems. He'd long ago given up reading any press about JMH. That is, until today. In a childish action that matched his mood, he tossed his bike helmet on the couch, knowing that bugged Nana.

"There you are." Nana walked in drying her hands on a dish towel. She eyed the helmet on the couch. "Did you and Autumn go for a ride? It's a beautiful evening, now that it's cooled down."

"No, I went by myself." He ran his hand over his hair. "How are you feeling?"

"Fine. It was only a headache from the heat. I hope Autumn didn't make it out to be more. Are you hungry or did you stop for something while you were out? We could have sandwiches and some of the potato salad from yester-day." She danced around the elephant in the room.

"Nana, please, sit." He dropped onto the couch next to his helmet. "What's going on?"

She twisted the towel. "I didn't mean for you to find out that way. We just made the offer. I don't know how the newspaper got wind of it."

He patted the seat and she walked over and joined him. "Explain *it*."

"After you asked me if I knew anything about your grandfather having designs on buying your birthing center…"

His birthing center again. He swallowed, remembering that's what he'd said when he'd talked with his grandfather.

Nana folded the dish towel in her lap. "I'd had the thought in my head since shortly after I came up here and saw how well you're doing. I called the daughter of a friend of mine who's involved with raising venture capital and had her do some investigating for me."

So that's why she'd seemed to be holding back when he'd first asked her about Grandfather buying the birthing center.

She patted the towel. I have all that money from my parents and time is running out to use it. I'm not young anymore, and your parents certainly don't need it. The financial advisor and I put together the offer to Adirondack Medical Center." The smile she gave him radiated pride.

That was something, but it didn't answer the big question. "Why?"

"For you, of course."

"I don't understand."

"The birthing center is in financial trouble. You must know that. You are the director."

He nodded.

"You seem to like it here. You've made friends."

"Yes, but what does that have to do with buying the center?"

Nana shook out the towel and refolded it. "It was probably only a matter of time before your grandfather and JMH set their eyes on your center."

Jon was still having trouble putting the pieces together. He drilled his gaze into hers. "Which, according to the newspaper article, they did. How is Grandfather involved? Did you really put together the offer yourself or did Grandfather make you? Did he want the center and need you and your friends to finance it?" He shot his questions at her.

She pulled back from him and hurt shone in her eyes. "I invited him in on the deal as part of a reconciliation."

Jon stared at her.

"Don't look at me like that. I was going to go back to him eventually. I have nearly sixty years of my life invested in him and our marriage." Her voice dropped. "And I love him."

Jon shrunk into the couch back, sorry about bombarding her with questions and his reaction to her reconciling with Grandfather. That was her business and he respected that, as Nana had always respected his decisions without trying to manipulate him to her way like his parents and grandfather.

"I still don't understand how I fit in. After the takeover, I'm sure Grandfather's first move will be to fire me as director and put in one of his people."

"Jonathan Mitchell Hanlon." Nana punctuated each syllable of his name with a wave of her finger. "While you and your grandfather have your differences, he's not the devil incarnate you make him out to be, which is why he agreed he and JMH would be a silent partner. My investor group wants to be able to call on his experience without applying his usual business model to the center."

"When I called, he told me that he's only a silent partner. I didn't believe him. He also refused to give me any informa-

tion about the takeover, said to ask you and hung up on me."
In his frustration, Jon didn't care if he sounded like a petu-
lant child.

"His people skills aren't the best. One of the reasons he
needs me." She touched his hand. "He's happy to have you in
on this family venture. Trust me."

He pushed against the old longing to have family ties that
didn't come with strings attached. "Good to know I won't be
out of a job. I hope the rest of my staff won't be either." His
thoughts went to Autumn and the new position he'd
requested.

"Staffing would be up to you as director, and your new
contract would have stock options to give you an ownership
interest in the center."

He froze at stock options. It was as if Nana were trying to
tie him to the center for some reason. Autumn? Although
Nana obviously liked her, he couldn't see his grandmother
going to such extremes to play matchmaker. Nor did she
have to.

"Nana. What aren't you telling me?"

"I thought you'd be happy with my helping you do what
you want to do, like when I helped you with medical school.
Brad was right."

Brad? Jon rubbed his temples. What did Angie's husband
have to do with this? If he didn't know his grandmother had
been instrumental in putting together a major business
buyout, he'd be concerned about senility.

"You don't intend to stay at the center. You never did.
You really do plan to go to Haiti." Nana's voice grew quieter
with each word and Jon's temperature rose.

She wanted to buy the birthing center to keep him from
going to Haiti? A pain split his head that no amount of
rubbing his temples would relieve. Nana didn't do that. She
didn't use money to manipulate him. That was the realm of

his parents and grandfather. While Grandfather was involved, he wasn't the instigator this time.

"You knew that. I told you I'd been called to serve in Haiti." Jon tapped down his disappointment and anger to keep his tone even.

Nana's eyes glistened with unshed tears. "I thought you'd change your mind once you found a position you liked that would let you practice the way you want, among people who needed you. I thought you'd found that here."

He had in a lot of ways. But he still felt compelled to go to Haiti and help set up a better program of maternal care so Angie's death wouldn't seem so senseless. He believed that was his calling. To be there for the women of Haiti who, like Angie, needed his medical expertise and had no one else to provide it.

"I wanted to keep the center open so you wouldn't lose what you've found. When Angie's husband mentioned that you'd applied to Help for Haiti and plan to leave when your contract in Ticonderoga is up next year, I got scared. I lost Angie. I can't lose you, too."

Now she *was* being irrational. "You're not going to lose me if I go serve in Haiti." He took a breath. "You could lose me if you use your money to manipulate me."

"I'm not doing that. I didn't mean to do that. I simply wanted to give you the support your parents never have. I'm an old woman. Forgive me if I've hurt you. I mean well."

He hugged her. "Of course I forgive you."

And I hope you—and Autumn—will forgive me for what I have to do.

NANA WAS GONE when he got up the next morning. She'd left him a note saying she'd gone to church and would be leaving right after to go visit Grandfather. She hadn't mentioned the visit yesterday. He hoped his silent treatment last night hadn't caused her to leave. There hadn't been anything more to say after their evening talk. He was glad that the note said she was picking up his youngest cousin from college in Schenectady to share the drive downstate. Westchester County was a long drive from Paradox Lake for someone Nana's age.

He rubbed his eyes and looked at the kitchen clock again. 10:15, which shouldn't be such a surprise since he hadn't fallen asleep until sometime after 3:20. He needed to talk with Autumn. Tell her what he'd found out from Nana. See if talking with someone else could dispel the emptiness inside him that had kept him awake most of the night.

The light on the coffee maker was off, so the half pot on the burner was most likely cold. He poured a cup anyway and stuck it in the microwave. *Something physical might help.* He peered out the window. By the looks of the gray clouds moving in, he should have just enough time to run his usual route around the lake before Autumn got home from church and the rain started. His heart thumped in trepidation about facing Autumn.

AUTUMN WATCHED Jon out of her window, something she'd found herself doing all too often. He jogged up the front walk and hesitated a moment before taking the Y to his door, allowing her a nice view of his t-shirt plastered across his chest. No one, not even her, could argue that the man wasn't beautiful.

She went upstairs and was in the middle of making her bed when a knock sounded at the door. Her breath caught.

Jon with the information about the birthing center? She ran downstairs.

"Hey," he said through the screen looking every bit as handsome in the dry polo shirt he'd changed into as he did in his t-shirt.

"Hey, yourself. Come on in."

He let himself in and stood by the door. "I talked with Grandfather and Nana about the birthing center sale. Nana was the one with more information."

Her chest tightened. Was that why Mrs. Hanlon had acted strangely when she'd gone over yesterday to find Jon? She knew about the takeover? But she'd told Jon before that she hadn't. "Sit down."

He strode over and lowered himself onto the couch. She sat in the chair across from him on a premonition she'd want to have some space between them when he shared what he'd found out.

"Nana is one of the individual investors on the buyout deal. In fact, she put it together." He leaned back and studied her.

She wasn't going to let him disarm her with his slow, steady perusal. This was her livelihood they were talking about. "Why? And what about JMH?" she shot back.

"JMH is involved for its and Grandfather's expertise. And as part of a reconciliation between Nana and Grandfather. JMH is a minor, supposedly silent, partner."

"Your grandmother is buying the birthing center in order to reconcile with your grandfather?" She knew that Jon's family moved in a different world than she and her family did, but what Jon had said still sounded crazy to her.

His shoulders slumped. "No, she put the buyout deal together for me."

That made no more sense than what he'd said about his grandparents.

"I'm not doing this very well," he said with a lopsided grin that went straight to her heart.

"No, you're not."

"I'll start over." He explained what he'd learned from his grandmother. "She and Grandfather, so she says, thought the buyout was a good way to bring me back into the family." He leaned forward, elbow on knees. "You have to understand that with my family, business and career is all there is. They think you can buy love." His voice dropped. "They're not like your family, except Nana."

His grandmother's going in with his grandfather to buy Jon a medical facility sounded like she ascribed to the "buy love" philosophy, too. At least in part. "This is your family's way of reconciling. Your grandmother and grandfather and your grandfather and you?"

"As strange as it sounds, yes. And Nana wanted to keep me at the center."

Finally, something that Autumn could understand. If JMH alone or another health care corporation took over the center, Jon very well could be asked to leave so they could appoint their own director. With his grandmother's deal, the center could stay open with Jon as director. Her mind jumped to the staff position Jon had all but offered her. Joy filled her. She and Jon could continue to practice at the center, stay in Paradox Lake. Together with the rest of the current staff, they could model the center as the caring facility they both wanted.

"But I can't stay."

Autumn jerked up in the chair. "You're leaving?"

He dropped his head in an almost-imperceptible nod. "I signed a one-year contract with Adirondack Medical intending to leave when the contract is up and serve with Help for Haiti for a year or two."

A sense of betrayal immobilized Autumn. But Jon didn't

owe any loyalty to the center beyond the terms of his contract. Her stomach churned. Or to her, really. As much as she wanted it, their feelings for each other were too new to bind them.

"Now, I'll have to leave sooner. Nana admitted that she did all this to keep me from going to Haiti. She has an irrational fear that she'll lose me like she lost Angie. I can't let her, however well-meaning her intentions, manipulate me, keep me from my calling to serve in Haiti any more than I could accept my parents' and grandfather's machinations to make me become a surgeon." He opened his hands, palms out toward her. "I'm committed to using my training to do everything I can to protect other women, families, from the facing the tragedy Angie's did, to do my part to right her death. And I'm called to do that work in Haiti."

"You're sure it's a calling and not unresolved grief?" She knew it was a self-centered question. But the dynamics of the birthing center, her involvement there, would change if Jon left. His grandmother might rescind the buyout offer. The center could close. Her life—professional and personal —would change dramatically.

"It's what I believe."

He hadn't really answered her question.

"I know this sounds selfish. Paradox Lake is your home. But come with me to Haiti. We work so well together. Think of how much we have to offer, what we could give to women who really need our help—give free from the politics of the birthing center sale, free from JMH."

Her heart skipped a beat. Was this Jon's way of making a commitment?

"You wouldn't have to serve as a midwife. They have as great a need for delivery nurses."

That wasn't why she was hesitating to respond. "Haiti is a long way from Paradox Lake, from my family and friends."

"You'd only have to sign on for a year."

"I'll think about it. But to be honest, I'm not sure that's my calling." She ignored the pang that struck her heart. "There's a great need for medical care here in the Adirondacks, and my dream has always been to practice right here at home."

"Your dream or what your family expects of you?" he gently challenged her. "They've all stayed here or come back to Paradox Lake. That doesn't mean you have to."

"I know. And I have lived elsewhere." And when she had, she'd always wanted to come back to the Adirondacks. Maybe she should think about why.

"People can manipulate with love as much as they manipulate with money."

She stared at him, a sadness enveloping her. "My family's love isn't manipulative. Dad and Gram and Gramps and everyone else give it freely. No one is tying me to Paradox Lake with their expectations. In fact, back when I was in high school, Aunt Jinx did everything she could to get me to go away to college. *I*"—she emphasized the word—"truly love it here."

Defeat marred his handsome features, which tore at her heart. He was asking her to make a choice she didn't want to be forced to make. And she wanted to ask the same of him.

CHAPTER 16

utumn was still wrestling with her decision about Haiti a week later when she arrived at the birthing center for her Monday afternoon appointment with a new expectant mother. The starlit cruise of Lake George with Jon had almost induced her to say yes. She'd retreated to undecided in the days since.

Jon had been so busy with meetings at the medical center in Saranac Lake about the sale, appointments, and deliveries that they'd barely seen each other. So, she'd asked Kari to check Jon's schedule this morning to see if he was available at lunch time and packed the surprise picnic she had in the basket on her arm.

"Hi," she said to the receptionist. "Is Dr. Hanlon in?"

The woman looked at the picnic basket and grinned.

Ah, the birthing center grapevine at work.

"No, he's not back from Saranac Lake yet."

Kari hadn't said anything about him having a meeting at the medical center this morning.

"Autumn." Jon's voice sounded behind her. "Just the person I'm looking for."

She felt herself blush at the enthusiasm in his words and what the receptionist might be thinking.

"I have some good news." He reached for the picnic basket. "I'll take that for you."

She let him. "I made us a picnic lunch to have before your afternoon appointments."

"Perfect. Come on down to my office."

Autumn felt the receptionist's gaze on her as they walked down the hall, but she didn't care.

Jon put the basket on the table in his office and Autumn spread out the food. "What's your good news?"

"I got a call from the director at Help for Haiti first thing this morning."

Autumn stilled with the plate she was holding hovering midway between the basket and the table.

"He said the organization had received an unexpected large donation and has the funding for us to go as soon as next month."

"Us? You told him about me?"

"Sure, right after I'd invited you to come with me. I sent him your vitae that's on file here at the center. He said they can always use nurses and midwives."

She placed the plate on the table before she dropped it. "What did you tell him this morning?" Dread filled her.

"That we accept. He's sending the job offers for us to review. He'll be calling to interview you after I let him know I've told you. It's just a formality," he assured her.

"Just like that? Without asking me? I haven't made my decision." *Or maybe I have now.*

His eyes narrowed. "What do you mean? The cruise on Lake George…"

"I said I was leaning toward going to Haiti. I didn't say I'd actually decided." Apparently, Jon had heard what he wanted to hear.

"It probably won't be as soon as next month, if that's your concern."

She steeled her heart against the plea in his voice.

"When I tendered my resignation at the medical center this morning, I agreed to stay at the birthing center until they or the new birthing center owners found someone to replace me."

"You resigned? You're going whether I am or not?" She choked the words out.

Confusion clouded his face. "I thought you understood. I made a commitment to myself to do this."

But not a commitment to her. How foolish of her to open her heart to Jon, to think he'd changed his love-them-and-leave-them ways. Except in her case, it wasn't for another woman, but for a shadow from his past.

A knock sounded on the door, and it cracked open. Kari stuck her head in. "Sorry to interrupt you. Kelly was called to a birth and needs you to cover her 12:30 appointment."

"That's okay," Autumn said. "We're finished." As she stood to leave, she avoided looking at Jon to see if he'd gotten her full meaning.

His "I'll talk to you later" said he didn't, adding to her hurt. He didn't know or care to know her at all. The tentative foundation she'd built for a meaningful relationship with him crumbled.

"What's wrong?" Kari asked as soon as they were in the hall.

"Nothing I can't handle." *With time.*

CHAPTER 17

"*D*r. Hanlon." Kari intercepted him on his way to his office. "We have a problem."

"I have some time free. Come with me to my office." Maybe he could find out from Kari where Autumn was. She wasn't at the duplex, and he'd been trying to call her for the past three days. Her cell phone went directly to voice mail. They needed to talk, straighten out what had gone wrong between them on Monday. He needed to make her see that his commitment to going to Haiti didn't mean he didn't care about her and their possible future together. His chest tightened. If she couldn't understand, she didn't understand him, and there was no future for them.

"No, I'm fine," Kari said. "I don't have a problem. It's one of our mothers. She's arrived in active, rather late, labor. It's her fourth and she wanted to 'get the house in order' before the birth."

"Kelly's with her?"

"No, that's the problem. Kelly is in Syracuse with her daughter at college orientation. Maureen was supposed to cover this birth if it happened while Kelly was away. But she broke her ankle sliding into home at her softball game last night."

"You want me to cover. That's no problem."

"No," Kari insisted. "It is a problem. It's one of our families from the traditional By His Word church community south of Schroon Lake. They don't believe men, other than a husband, should be at a birth." She gave him a pointed look. "She's far enough along that I don't think we have time to send them to Dr. Craven in Saranac Lake."

"We won't need to do that. I'll come and talk with them. I know the families prefer a midwife or female doctor, but there isn't one available. So they're stuck with me. What else can they do?"

Kari shook her head in doubt and said something under her breath that sounded like, "You'd be surprised."

"Are they in your office or a birthing suite?" he asked.

"The office. The family wanted a home birth but agreed to a center birth if Kelly wasn't available and Maureen had to do the birth. I think they hoped Autumn would be catching babies again by the time the baby was born. Like I'm hoping." She grinned. "No offense."

"None taken, and I'm sure Autumn wants to be at your birth either way." He turned and headed for the midwifery office. When he entered, his gaze immediately went to the very pregnant mother-to-be. Like the other mother from the traditional church community he'd seen in the midwives' office earlier in the summer, she was dressed in a calf-length navy blue skirt and a three-quarter-length-sleeve white maternity t-shirt. The two little girls with her had on sun dresses with t-shirts underneath. Her husband had his arm protectively around her waist. A boy older than the girls stood on her other side.

"Hi." Jon extended his hand to the father. "I'm Dr. Hanlon."

"I'm Daniel Murray, and this is my wife, Ruth, and Matthew, Miriam and Leah."

"Nice to meet you all." He looked at Ruth. "Let's get you down to one of the birthing suites."

"You've gotten a hold of Autumn?" Ruth glanced from Jon to Kari.

"No, we haven't," Kari said. "I've left a message on her home phone and her cell. I'm afraid she's somewhere out of cell phone service range."

"We'll go home and wait for her," the man said.

"Your wife is in labor. You can't." Jon corrected himself. "You shouldn't do that."

"Birth is a natural process," the mother said. "I've already had three normal deliveries."

Jon positioned himself to block the door. His cousin Angie's face flashed in his mind. "Yes. Even so, unexpected complications can present."

"You can't stop them," Kari mouthed over the boy's head.

Jon knew he had no legal standing to stop them. There were no laws against unassisted births. "Kari, why don't you go to their home and wait with Daniel and Ruth until Autumn can get there."

Kari's eyes widened.

"I'd like you to," Ruth said.

"But only if you're comfortable with that," Jon added.

Kari avoided his gaze and looked directly at the mother. "Yes, I will. I need to talk with Dr. Hanlon, and I'll be right over."

Jon moved aside and the family filed out.

"What are you thinking?" Kari demanded as soon as the door closed behind them. "You all but promised Autumn would come for the birth."

He ignored her question. "Where *is* Autumn? I haven't seen her car at the duplex the past couple of days."

"I don't know for sure. She told Kelly that she needed to take a few days off to think."

Jon locked his jaw. He had a good idea of what she had to think about. Going to Haiti. How he'd tramped ahead and arrogantly assumed that if he went to Haiti, she would, too.

"You don't have any idea where I can get a hold of her?" he asked.

"Sorry, I don't. You have her father's home number, don't you? Try him." Kari started moving around the office to gather things to take with her to the Murrays'. "I need to go. They'll have the baby whether any of us are there to help with the delivery or not," she said as she left.

Her words squeezed all of the air out of his lungs. *Like Angie.* He scrolled through his contacts on his cell phone and found Neal's number. Leaning his shoulder against the wall outside his office, Jon counted the rings as he waited.

"Hello." A woman answered the phone.

"Mrs. Hazard? Jon Hanlon. Do you know where Autumn is? How I can get in touch with her?"

"She's right here."

He wiped his brow. He hadn't expected to find her so easily. But he should have. Of course, she'd go to her family.

"Autumn," Anne's voice came over the phone from a distance. "It's Jon."

"Jon?" Autumn said when she took the phone.

"Where have you been? Kari and I have been trying to get a hold of you." He cringed. His voice sounded so harsh. But they were and he had been for days.

"On vacation." Dead silence followed her statement.

Jon checked to make sure he hadn't lost his connection.

"Is something wrong?" she asked.

"Ruth Murray is in labor, late-stage labor. Her husband brought her into the center, and they left when they found out I was the only one available to deliver the baby."

"Where's Maureen? She's our cover."

"She broke her ankle last night, and Dr. Craven is in Saranac today. I sent Kari over to the Murrays' house about a half hour ago. I need you to go, too."

"You want me to deliver the baby?"

"What other choice do we have?" He slapped himself in the side of the head. What an idiot he was to say it that way. "That came out badly. But I keep thinking about my cousin and how no one was there to help her when she needed it."

He could hear the background noise of the Hazard household, even though Autumn was quiet, so he knew they were still connected. Was she thinking about the friends she'd told him about, the birth that had made her give up deliveries? "I'll come, too," he assured her. "And Kari will be with you. You won't be alone."

"Someone should be there. It's not fair to put the responsibility on Kari."

"Think of Lisa. You could have done that birth without me," he said. "No sweat. And how well we worked together with Christie."

"You know Daniel and Ruth probably won't let you in the bedroom for the delivery, even if there's a problem."

"It doesn't matter. You don't need me."

"You really believe that, don't you?"

He did. She didn't need him to deliver the baby. Nor, he suspected, did she need him in her life the way he needed her. He'd really messed things up.

"Yes. Now get over to Daniel and Ruth's house and catch that baby. I'll be there as quickly as I can."

"You have directions?"

Was Autumn stalling? No, she wouldn't. "Yes, Kari gave them to me."

"Okay, then, I'll see you in about 20 minutes."

"Right." Except that, as she'd just reminded him, he probably wouldn't be seeing Autumn until after the baby was born.

AUTUMN BREATHED DEEPLY in an attempt to calm the turbulence inside her. She could do this. She had to do this. As she gathered what she needed, she repeated, "You can do it."

When she arrived at the Murray's house their Matthew, let her in, and she explained that Jon would be arriving in a few minutes.

"Do you know who he is, so you'll recognize him?"

"Yes, I remember him from this afternoon. I wouldn't answer the door if it was a stranger. Why's he coming if you're here?"

Because she was afraid. Because he could take over if she panicked and couldn't do it. Because she just plain needed him and his strength. "He's my friend," she said.

The boy shrugged her answer off.

"Autumn. I thought I heard your voice." Kari stood on the open stairway. "I'm glad you're here."

"Is something wrong?" Fear crushed the air from her lungs.

"No." Kari narrowed her eyes and jerked her head toward the kids. "Everything's going well."

The weight on her chest lifted and she breathed in the breath she'd lost. "What are we waiting for? Let's go upstairs so I can check on your work."

"You'll find it stellar as always." Kari stopped at the top of the stairs. "And to answer your earlier question, I'm glad you're here because you need the experience. You may be a little rusty, and I want you up to speed when this one is born." Kari patted her belly.

Right. She had to get through this birth first. Then, who knew if she'd even be here in Paradox Lake when Kari's baby was born.

JON ARRIVED at the house about a half hour later. "I'm Dr. Hanlon," he said when Matthew opened the door.

"Yeah, Autumn said you were coming."

"Can you help me get some things from my car?"

He and Matthew unloaded the portable oxygen tank and extra medications. Jon looked around the comfortable living room of the old farmhouse. Matthew's sisters were playing a board game on the braided rug on the floor. The house was quiet. Too quiet? Had something gone wrong? He pushed that thought from his mind.

"Please let Autumn know I'm here."

"Sure." The boy went upstairs and came back with Autumn.

Jon searched her face for tension and relaxed when he saw none. "You didn't need to come down. I take it everything is going well."

"Ruth is in the shower, so I'm not really needed at the moment." She rubbed the back of her neck as if it were tight.

Maybe he'd misread her. "I brought extra oxygen and meds if they're needed."

She shook her head. "I doubt it. We're almost there, nearing transition. I expect we'll see the wee one in the next hour or so."

"You holding up okay?"

"Yes. Good," she said. "Better than good." She reached between them and took his hands in hers and squeezed them. "Excited."

His heart swelled. This was the Autumn he remembered

from his residency days at Samaritan. The woman who gloried in each birth as if it were her first. "Super." He squeezed her hands back and her light blue eyes went smoky. "I'm sorry," he blurted.

Her eyes narrowed. "Pardon?"

If he wanted any possibility of a future with Autumn, he owed her an apology for the way he'd pressed ahead without talking to here again and accepted both offers from Help for Haiti. "About Haiti. The way I handled it." He cleared his throat. "I didn't consider you . . . your . . ."

"No, you didn't."

She wasn't making this any easier for him. He smiled. She pressed her lips together and shook her head. *Bad idea*. What was he thinking? The Hanlon charm had never worked on her before. Why would it now?

"I got caught up in the idea of going to Haiti, of our going to Haiti." He raised his hands in supplication.

"I can understand that, getting carried away with the excitement of realizing something you want."

His pulse quickened. "Then, you can forgive me?"

The corner of her mouth quirked up. "I'll take it under consideration."

He leaned forward, forgetting the distance he'd put between them with his rash action concerning Help for Haiti and that they weren't alone.

"Hey, it's my turn, not yours," Miriam said.

"No, you just played," Leah shot back.

The girls' voices arguing over their game brought him back from the emotional haze that surrounded him and Autumn.

He straightened and Autumn pulled her hands from his. "I'm glad you're here on my team," she said in a soft voice, "even if you have to stay downstairs."

"Autumn," Kari called. "Can you come up here?"

Jon tensed, analyzing the nurse's tone for any sign of a problem.

"I'd better go," Autumn said. "Babies wait for no one."

"Isn't that the truth. You'll let me know if you need me?"

She nodded, and he watched her disappear upstairs. After listening to the muffled voices above, he began pacing the living room. He stopped at the front window and stared out into the fading evening sun. When Jon turned, Matthew looked up from the book he was reading.

"Dr. Hanlon, do you want to sit down? I can put on a movie or something."

"I'm good," Jon said.

"Well, you're making me kind of nervous." Matthew rose and motioned Jon to the kitchen. "Is something wrong with Mom? What did Autumn say?"

"No, Autumn said everything was fine."

The boy looked skeptical.

Autumn *had* said everything was fine. Still, he was worrying and making Matthew worry.

"You're not just saying that, are you?"

"I'm not just saying that," Jon answered in a tired voice. Then it hit him. He looked for a problem in every birth he attended, was always alert for something to go wrong. He'd gone into obstetrics not to birth babies, as Autumn had, but to save women from complications of childbirth, even those who didn't need to be "saved." He went completely still. For the first time, he questioned whether his calling to service in Haiti was actually a calling.

"Excuse me." A woman Jon didn't recognize stood in the kitchen doorway with the two little girls. "I'm Ruth's mother. We came to get Matthew. It's almost time for him to cut the cord."

Jon's heart lightened. That was good news.

"Okay, Grandma." Matthew looked up at Jon. "Cutting the cord is my birth job. We all have one."

Of course, the boy had a birth job. That fell right in line with Autumn's family-centered care. "See," Jon said silently to Matthew's departing back, "everything is fine."

Jon returned to the now empty living room, stepped over the girls' abandoned game, and walked upstairs. He needed to be as close to Autumn as he could be to celebrate the moment in spirit if not by his physical presence. When he got to the top of the stairs, he saw the bedroom door was ajar, giving him a side view of Autumn and Daniel. He crept closer, justifying that he was wasn't violating the family's wishes because he couldn't see Ruth.

"I need to push," she said.

"Let me take a look," Autumn said bending out of view. "Wait."

"Is something wrong?" Daniel asked, voicing the words that sprang to Jon's mind.

"The baby's breech, coming feet first. She must have flipped since Ruth's last visit with Kelly."

Jon's thoughts warred with each other. Autumn hadn't checked Ruth's progress before now? He would have. But other midwives and doctors wouldn't have. His mouth went dry. Had Autumn delivered a breech baby before? He hadn't. Not naturally, only by C-section. If Autumn saw the feet, they didn't have time to get Ruth to the hospital in Saranac Lake. It was also too late for an emergency C-section. There was nothing he could do.

"I really need to push." A tone of desperation laced Ruth's voice.

"Matthew was breech," Daniel said. "Kelly delivered him right here."

"Yes. I've done this before," Ruth said.

At least someone had, Jon thought. He took a step forward

before stopping himself from barging into the room and telling Autumn she could handle it. His presence wouldn't do anything to help.

"Go ahead," Autumn said in a surprisingly neutral tone.

Jon tensed and clenched his fists with each sound Ruth made.

"That's it," Daniel encouraged his wife. "Her legs are out."

A loud groan followed his pronouncement.

"She's a he. It's a boy." Daniel's voice rose in excitement.

"Yes!" Matthew's voice came from another part of the room, and Jon could picture him shooting his arm into the air and fist pumping.

Jon waited for the baby's wail. His heart stopped when he didn't hear it.

"He's not crying." Ruth's voice trembled. "Is he okay?"

Autumn lifted the baby toward Ruth and out of his sight and leaned forward. She and Kari must be resuscitating him. Jon counted, one, two, three, four...fifty-five, fifty-six, fifty-seven. *Come on!* A loud cry broke the silence. "Thank God," he whispered.

Autumn straightened back into view. "You can cut the cord now, Matthew."

The radiance on her face as she watched lit his heart. He stood in awe. Unlike Autumn, he'd never been free to simply celebrate the gift of life. And, although his part had been small, he was glad to have been a part of bringing that joy back to her. It was the least he could do.

He slipped back downstairs before anyone saw him and stood at the window viewing the bright pinpoints of light the stars made in the clear night sky. Witnessing the birth, knowing there was nothing he could do to help Autumn, was humbling. About twenty minutes later, he heard water running upstairs. He was sitting on the couch leafing through a hunting and fishing magazine when Autumn and Kari came down.

"Hey," Autumn greeted him, her face still aglow. We're giving the family time to get acquainted with their new son."

Jon stood and put the magazine down on an end table. "A boy to even things up." He walked over to Autumn.

"Exactly what Matthew thought. You were so quiet down here," Autumn said. "I wondered if you'd left."

Guilt pinched him for a second as he thought about his stealing upstairs. "Not a chance." His voice sounded thick to his ears.

"We did it." Autumn gazed up at him.

"No, you did it," he replied.

"I think I'll go make that tea, Autumn," Kari said, reminding him that he and Autumn weren't alone. "And take mine out on the back deck and look at the stars."

"Yes, the tea," Autumn said. "Leave the water and I'll have some, too."

Kari grinned at him from behind Autumn and gave him a thumbs-up sign.

"How are you?"

"Great," Autumn said. "It was beautiful. I couldn't have asked for a better birth experience, even if it was touch and go for a minute."

"I know."

Autumn tilted her head and looked sidewise at him. "You know?"

"You were awesome. I don't know if I could have handled it as well as you did. I've never done a natural breech birth." Jon explained how he'd been upstairs in the hall, rushing on before she could find fault with his action. "It was beautiful. You were beautiful." His voice grew husky. "You are beautiful."

He pulled her into his arms and kissed her. She returned

his kiss with a fervor that he hoped was really for him and not simply a release of adrenalin built up during the birth.

"I couldn't have done it without you, your believing in me, pushing me," she whispered against his lips.

He loosened his embrace. "Yes, you could have. Maybe not this birth, but another sometime in the future."

"Thank you anyway, for being on my team."

"It's a winning team," he said, "the only type I belong to."

Autumn laughed. "Me, too."

He took her hand and led her to the couch. "Sit. I have something to say, something I was thinking about after the birth when I was looking out at the stars."

"This sounds serious." Her eyes twinkled.

"It is." He couldn't remember the last time he'd felt so self-conscious with a woman. But Autumn wasn't just any woman. "We make a great team on the job. And off the job, too. Can we go back to Monday morning before I got stupid?"

She stared at him, and his heart froze. She wasn't going to forgive him? Where were those smooth words that used to come easily to his tongue? He swallowed. They'd come easily because his heart hadn't been involved with any other woman. With Autumn, he needed straight words.

"I care for you, may be falling in love with you. I think you care for me." *Or had*. He prayed she still did.

"I do." Her delicate features softened. "But I needed to know your commitment to Help for Haiti didn't preclude your making a commitment to me, to us."

His heart skipped two beats. "I think we could have something real and lasting."

"Even though you're going to Haiti?" she asked.

"Even if I go to Haiti." He caught his "if" only after he'd said it.

"Even if I don't go to Haiti?" she pressed.

He slipped his arm around her shoulders, and she placed her head on his shoulder. "Real love can weather a separation, if necessary. I want to see if we can build that kind of love."

She nestled a little closer. "I'm game if you are."

EPILOGUE

Three months later

"Haiti or Bust" the multi-colored banner strung across the Hazardtown Fire Hall proclaimed to everyone who entered. Autumn stood behind the serving window in the kitchen and cast an eye over the crowd that had gathered for the luncheon to honor the doctor and nurse the hamlet was sponsoring through Help for Haiti. Jon slipped in beside her.

"We did it," she said, feeling a tingle of warmth that had nothing to do with the heat of the kitchen, the crowded hall, or her pride that the trivia group's project had raised enough money to send not one but two medical professionals to Haiti.

"And then some, thanks to the efforts of the male contingent of the fundraisers," he teased.

She rolled her eyes. "Will I never hear the end of it? You only pulled ahead because your grandfather signed the check from your grandmother, and the fundraiser's treasurer logged it for the male team. The treasurer who just happens to be a man."

Jon draped his arm across her shoulders and squeezed her to his side. "He was only calling things as he saw them. And sexist as it might be, most of the support from the Volunteer Fire Department was male because most of the volunteers are male. Their contribution is the one that put us over our goal."

She leaned her head against his shoulder. Once Jon had caught on that competition could be friendly, he'd taken up the gauntlet with both hands. She supposed it was only right that his team had won, even if it was on a technicality.

The guests of honor entered the hall to a round of applause. Dr. Michaels and his wife, Leigh, would save countless lives, as Jon wanted. As they all wanted. The fire chief led them to the head table. Jon watched with a serious, almost longing expression that made her start.

"Do you regret your decision?"

His gaze remained focused on the head table. "We could have done a lot of good."

He'd said that he no longer felt a calling to serve in Haiti himself and had spent much of the last three months in sometimes acrimonious negotiations with his grandfather working out his multi-year contract to direct the newly sold birthing center. The center's buyers had appointed his grandfather to represent them in all of the sale negotiations.

Although Adirondack Medical Center had accepted his resignation, they hadn't actively searched for a replacement. They'd left that to the new owners, who'd had an offer ready when Jon had decided not to go to Haiti. The offer he'd renegotiated with his grandfather. Jon had driven down to Westchester to sign the contract yesterday, returning late last night, so she hadn't had a chance to ask how it had gone.

He squeezed her to his side. "And you'll do a lot of good here as the new assistant director of the birthing center."

Autumn checked the squeal that rose in her throat. "Are

you serious?" She'd hoped for a midwife position on the center staff. Assistant director was unbelievable.

He nodded and she waited for his familiar self-satisfied grin to break across his face. Her heart dropped when it didn't.

"Grandfather wanted to bring in one of his people. For balance, he said. He also accused me of letting my personal feelings color my business decisions. I set him straight on that."

Of course he did. For Jon, business was still all business. But she chose to believe his feelings for her had played at least a small part in his defense of choosing her as assistant director. Even if he didn't realize it.

"I needed a guarantee that someone would be in control at the center to carry out our vision if I wasn't."

Autumn slipped out from under his arm. "But why wouldn't—"

"Here you are," her father interrupted. "We saved you two seats at our table. If you don't come and take them right now, I can't guarantee we'll be able to hang on to them. I can't believe the turnout."

"We'd better take the man up on his offer," Jon said. "I wouldn't want to miss out on lunch because I have no place to eat it."

He placed his hand at the small of her back and they followed her father through the maze of tables that had been set up in the hall. The pleasure of his nearness and the proprietary expression on his face washed away her question about why he was concerned with not being at the birthing center.

"I found them hiding in the kitchen," Dad proclaimed to the rest of her family, who were seated around the table shoulder to shoulder without an inch to spare.

"I was putting out the desserts," Autumn said.

"Sure you were," her aunt Jinx teased.

Autumn's cheeks warmed as she and Jon took the empty seats between her father and Aunt Jinx. Jon nudged his chair a half inch away from her father and closer to her, sending a thrill through her when he brushed her shoulder and leg with his. The slow smile that creased his face said he'd felt it, too.

As the meal progressed, Autumn noticed that, for someone who hadn't wanted to miss lunch, Jon was doing very little eating and a lot of pushing his food around on his plate and shooting furtive glances at the head table. In answer to one of Jon's glances, the fire chief gave him a solemn nod.

"I'd like everyone's attention, please." The chief paused until the luncheon chatter quieted. "I know we all enjoyed hearing Dr. Michaels and Leigh talk about Help for Haiti and their plans to serve the organization there, courtesy of our fundraising efforts."

The room broke into rousing applause.

The fire chief waited until it died down. "I'd like to give a special thanks to Autumn Hazard and Jon Hanlon for heading up our fundraising competition. We had a good time, didn't we? And we males dominated."

Laughs and more applause followed.

"Jon has asked to speak to you about some new plans he has."

The chief's eyes sparkled, and Autumn's stomach lurched. New plans that she didn't know about. Jon making provisions for the birthing center if he wasn't there. She couldn't throw off a fear that Jon had changed his mind and had decided to join Help for Haiti. While their relationship had blossomed in the past few months—she loved him—they hadn't made any verbal commitment to each other.

"Thanks." Jon stood, shifting his weight from foot to foot and avoiding Autumn's gaze.

She looked down at the table so no one would see the tears that pricked her eyes. If he needed to go to Haiti, she would survive, and if their newly forged love didn't, it would simply mean it wasn't a true love. She blinked. Even though she thought it was.

"As some of you know, when I came to Paradox Lake and the Ticonderoga Birthing Center earlier this year, I'd planned to only stay until my contract was up next summer and then go and serve with Help for Haiti. That was before Autumn came back into my life. So, I asked her to join me in serving with Help for Haiti."

Autumn's head shot up. That was settled months ago. He'd asked her, and she'd told him she couldn't, that her place was serving the people here in her hometown. Now he was going ask her again in front of all of her family and friends? Her answer was still the same. Yet why would he have negotiated with his grandfather to have her appointed assistant director of the center if he still wanted them to go to Haiti? Confusion filled the hollow in her stomach.

"Now." He cleared his throat and smiled the smile that made women's knees go weak. The smile she could no longer claim to be immune to. "We're about to undertake an even more life-changing journey right here in Paradox Lake...I hope," he added in a soft afterthought no one but she and her family could hear.

She crushed the paper napkin on her lap and her mind whirled with questions.

"And I couldn't think of a better place to announce it than here among family and friends."

Autumn followed Jon's gaze as he looked around their table and over to where his grandmother sat with his grand-father and her friends. Nana gave him a two-thumbs-up sign, and a hint of a smile showed on his grandfather's normally serious face.

Jon stepped away from his chair, dropped to one knee and reached in his suit coat pocket.

Autumn dropped the napkin on the floor.

He looked up at her, his eyes bright with a vulnerability she'd never seen before. "Autumn, I love you. Will you marry me?" He opened the jewelry box he'd pulled from his pocket.

"Oh!" All she could think was he wasn't leaving.

"No?" The look of despair on his handsome face was devastating.

"No…"

His despair deepened.

"I mean I said 'oh' not 'no.' You surprised me. Yes, yes, I'll marry you." She shot out of her seat and threw her arms around him. "I love you, too."

Above the cheers, someone started chanting, "kiss, kiss" until it became a room-wide buzz.

Autumn loosened her grip on Jon, and he bent his head to softly kiss her. "I'll finish this later in private," he whispered against her lips as he pulled away.

"I'll be looking forward to that."

He took the ring from the box and slipped it onto Autumn's finger. "We make a good team."

She held her hand out, so the ring glittered in the light. "The best. The very best."

∼

DEAR READER,

Thank you for reading *Trusting Love*. I hope you enjoyed Autumn and Jon's story. You can glimpse more of them and other characters from *Trusting Love* in my existing and upcoming Paradox Lake Sweet Romance stories.

Want to make sure you don't miss out on these and any of my other books and future releases? Sign up for my Readers Group Newsletter on my website. You'll receive a free book as a thank you. And I always appreciate when my readers take the time to leave an honest review of my books

JEAN

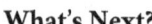

What's Next?

If you haven't read ***Trusting His Kiss: A Paradox Lake Novella*** yet you may want to. It's Autumn's delivery nurse Kari's story. You also meet the teenage Autumn.
And you have a chance to see more of teenage Autumn in her aunt Jinx's story ***Trusting Her Heart***

ABOUT THE AUTHOR

Jean C. Gordon's writing is a natural extension of her love of reading. From that day in first grade when she realized t-h-e was the word "the," she's been reading everything she can put her hands on. She and her college-sweetheart husband tried the city life in Los Angeles, but quickly returned home to their native small-town Upstate New York, where she sets many of her books. She and her husband share a 175-year-old farmhouse in Upstate New York with their daughter and her family.

Contact Jean on her website at JeanCGordon.com.

ALSO BY JEAN C. GORDON

More Team Macachek

Mending the Motocross Champion

Upstate NY...*where love is a little sweeter* Series

Bachelor Father

Love Undercover

Mandy and the Mayor

Candy Kisses

Mara's Move

Love Inspired

FRESH-START FAMILIES

Reuniting His Family

A Mom for His Daughter